DOCTOR

DOCTOR
in the GLEN

Sandy Young

British Library Cataloguing in Publication Data
A catalogue record of this book is available from the British Library

ISBN 1 899863 51 6

First published 1999
by House of Lochar

© Sandy Young 1999
© Cover illustration, Jill Dow 1999

Typeset by XL Publishing Services, Tiverton
Printed in Great Britain
by SRP Ltd, Exeter
for House of Lochar
Isle of Colonsay, Argyll PA61 7YR

CHAPTER 1

The hot, sultry African day melted into the darkness of the night as the big Masai sat cradling his toddler son at the entrance to his hut. The year was 1932. The panoply of stars was, on this evening, of little interest to Samuel MacLeod. All his attention was centred on the muted sounds coming from behind him.

Samuel had been abandoned as a baby and brought up by a missionary couple from an island called Lewis in far off Scotland. Being childless they had lavished much love on this small scrap of human flotsam who had come to them while clinging tenaciously to the last spark of life.

An urgency of noise brought him to his feet. Gently he laid the sleeping boy, Iain, on the ground and went in to where his wife lay on a rough bed. In the dim light of a paraffin lamp he could see sweat shining on her ebony forehead.

'Soon now, Samuel,' Naomi answered his unspoken question, then, 'go for Rebecca' she commanded sending him hurrying to another hut nearby.

When he returned with the older woman he gathered up his son and took him to her hut. There he eased him into bed beside her six year old grandson before resuming his vigil. Another hour crept gently away then a croon of voices from within was followed by a faint animal-like mew which, as Samuel hurried inside, became the lusty cry of a healthy baby.

'Are you all right, Naomi?' he asked as he dropped to his knees and grasped her hand. Her teeth shone white in the glow of the lamp as she smiled.

'I am well Samuel and so is our daughter,' she said. 'I now am the mother of a gentleman's family. Her name will be Ruth.'

Samuel choked back a sob of pleasure. He couldn't remember his own father who had been killed in a tribal dispute over grazing land. His mother had died soon afterwards of cholera compounded by a broken heart.

Rinderpest and the building of the Mombassa/Uganda railway through the heart of the Masai lands had decimated the cattle numbers. Years of senseless civil war between two factions of the tribe as to which were the true descendants of Olmasinta had led to the deaths of many of the fit young men on whom the weak depended to procure food. The death of Samuel's mother occurred in the middle of a drought. White settlers were moving in to the fertile highlands to the north of Nairobi. If the remnants of the tribe were to survive they had to trek south.

An orphan and sickly baby was an unnecessary impediment. He was going to die anyway as they would have to travel long distances each day. He was simply left behind. Fortunately a hunting party came by the following day, went through the empty huts in search of loot and found this infant who was still alive.

One of their leaders had been nursed back to health by the missionaries and they absolved their responsibility by taking the baby to the mission huts.

For upwards of a week his life hung by a thread. His stomach could only cope with small amounts of food at any one time, but constant care had its reward. The missionaries, whose name was MacLeod, decided to bring the boy up as the son whom they had never had. Until he was around four years of age they spoke to him in the Nilotic language of his own people.

He was a bright child who learned quickly. When they felt that he had a good grasp of that tongue they switched to their own native language which was Gaelic. It was a couple of years later that they began his education in English.

As is often the habit of a junior sibling, Ruth, from an early age, copied her brother in almost everything he did. The only brake on their wilder exploits was provided by their father.

Samuel had a gentle but strict upbringing and this he carried on to his children.

Although white settlement had meant the loss of land and altered the way of life of his ancestry, he harboured no resentment. Because the MacLeods had brought him up as their own son he understood the thought processes of the fiercely independent Scot and his name and soft-voiced Gaelic-based command of pure English was a passport into any company.

Even now when she was the mother of his two children, Naomi found it difficult to behave as his equal and abandon the normal subservience of an African wife. This was partly helped by their shared ambition for their children, but even so she tended to leave any application of strict discipline to her husband. The youngsters soon sensed this and that she disliked to see them 'skelped'. Samuel in his capacity as an elder had often to visit other villages to give advice and arbitrate in disputes and at times this meant a stay away from home of several nights. Any peccadilloes during these absences usually earned nothing more than a scolding from their mother and the threat of their father being told on his return. As this threat was never carried out, its deterrent effect was minimal.

Ruth was a toddler when Iain started to attend at the school compound and at first she had missed him terribly. They were both bright children and as they spent all the time that was possible together, babyhood was quickly replaced by mischievous childhood as she followed her older brother and hero.

One forenoon of a day when Samuel was away from home, Iain was at school and Naomi was mending clothes in the shade of the hut, Ruth played outside with a dog which belonged to one of the other huts in the kraal. The animal was good with children and Naomi allowed her mind to wander as she worked.

Samuel was increasingly being asked to arbitrate in disputes in other areas and his inability to refuse to help even in cases which took him away for several days was becoming a cause of friction between them. Naomi regretted her outbursts of temper and particularly so when people from other villages told her of the good work that he was doing.

But last night Ruth had come to bed in tears because her father hadn't been there to tuck her in. Naomi had expected him back and said that he would be there in the morning when the children awoke. Through a long sleepless night she had listened for footfall but it never came. When she found he wasn't there Ruth threw a tantrum.

'You told me a lie', she screamed as her small fists hammered at her mother's knees, 'you told me that Daddy would come back and he didn't. He's never coming back and it's your fault. I hate you,' she flung back as she ran outside.

Her mother felt a fierce stab of guilt. She was only too well aware that in the constricted and intimate confines of their small home the children must be aware of the quarrels between their parents. Her own childhood had been over-shadowed by tribal unrest. Each of her parents had had a brother contending for leadership of their tribe during the long illness of the old chief. In the end neither succeeded as both were killed during a dispute with the Masai over grazings. Now she, a Kikuyu, was married to a Masai whose own father had been killed in a similar dispute.

Her thoughts were suddenly brought into a sharp focus by the silence outside. Quickly she dropped her mending and moved out to the sun. The dog that Ruth had been playing with came forward to be petted, but there was no sign of the child. She shouted and other women emerged to join her. They all shook their heads in answer to her question. A quick search of all the huts was extended to other corners but revealed nothing.

At first Naomi felt only anxiety but this quickly gave way to fear. A fruitless half hour later, panic took hold. There were many dangers for a small child in the scrubby bush which grew right up to the edge of the compound and was tall and dense enough to conceal such a child from a foot searcher even at a distance of just a few yards. But there was nobody there to organise a search except for a few very old men and the women who were all mothers of children of their own. Of the able bodied men some were hunting and the rest were gathering cattle for dipping on a nearby farm. Where was Samuel? He was never here when his family needed him. He was always away looking after somebody else.

The voice of one of the old men saved her from developing hysteria.

'Rebecca has sent her daughter to the farm,' he said. 'The boss will come. He will bring men. They will find her. She cannot have gone far.'

The farmer was a Scot who had come to Kenya as a soldier during the 1914–18 war and had never gone home. He was a native Gaelic speaker named Roderick MacLean and, partly because of Samuel's knowledge of that language, but mainly because of mutual respect, the two men were as friendly as it was possible for two men of different colour to be anywhere in Africa at that time. The farm, most of which had been won from the bush through sheer hard work was called Ramasaig and he had explained to them that this was the name of the township, a Scottish Kraal as he said, where his people had lived for centuries before being moved out by an enforced migration called the Highland Clearances. The original Ramasaig was in the north-west corner of an island called Skye.

CHAPTER 2

About an hour had gone by before a sudden commotion announced the arrival of Roderick MacLean and two black men, all mounted on sweating horses. He immediately set about allaying Naomi's worst fears.

'We have been sweeping the bush for cattle since daylight,' he said. 'Any lion, hyena or other form of big cat will have been scared well away from here. We'll find the caileag bheag before long. Don't worry,' he flung over his shoulder as he brought his horse round in a tight turn and galloped off followed by his men.

But despite the optimism, Samuel arrived home in the afternoon to find his daughter still missing.

Paucity of sleep during the night coupled with anxiety had taken a heavy toll of Naomi and she clung to him for several moments before she could speak. When Iain came in from school he made little comment when his father explained the situation to him. Even when the horsemen came back, dusty and tired, to report failure and his father had made another comprehensive search of all likely places nearer to hand the boy took it all calmly.

Motivated more by the need to keep occupied than by hunger, Naomi prepared an evening meal of chicken and sweet potato and this with a sprinkle of marjoram as seasoning produced an extremely tempting smell. To her surprise, Samuel insisted that she set Ruth's place at the table and that a plate should be prepared as though she was there as usual. Naomi was puzzled but despite their increasing arguments she was accustomed to obeying her husband.

She was even more puzzled when, just after the three of them started their meal, the normally gentle and caring Samuel reached across to his daughter's place, lifted a piece of chicken, smelt it noisily and began to eat it with obvious relish. Then she looked at her son to see a large tear rolling down each of his cheeks.

Samuel rose and stretched out his hand.

'Come, Iain, take me to her, she must be hungry by now,' he said quietly.

Naomi sat at the table as the male members of her family passed out into the night. The sun had long since gone down but a three-quarter moon in a clear sky meant that after their eyes had adjusted their vision was good. At first their route lay over an area of scrub which Samuel realised was just tall enough to have given Ruth reasonable cover from chance eyes. They then came to an area of what the old MacLeods had called scutch grass and without hesitation Iain led his father toward what looked like impenetrable thorny bush at the foot of a sheer cliff which curved in the shape of an half-moon.

With the confidence of familiarity, the boy kept tight to the rock face then disappeared into a small black tunnel which had been formed by the natural curve of the branches. To follow, Samuel had to crawl on hands and knees. The thorn tore at his hair and gouged his shoulders but after a few yards he emerged in a grassy clearing. The slanting moon showed Iain standing at the mouth of a shallow cave. He was weeping uncontrollably.

Samuel rose to his feet and ran forward. His small daughter lay half turned on her side. A trail of vomit trickled from the side of her mouth. Her left foot was wedged behind a boulder which sat at the side of a rock. It was obvious from the unnatural angle that the shin bone was broken. The slight rise and fall of her chest showed that she was still alive. Mercifully, she was unconscious.

Samuel took a minute to comfort his son.

'Be brave, Iain, you'll have to help me. We must get her out of here.'

It required all his strength to move the boulder far enough to free the foot. He then took off his shirt and gently eased the small body inside it before binding the sleeves round her waist and tying them firmly. Next he went to the bushes and selecting a branch in the shape of the broken leg he broke it off and used a sharp stone to remove any thorns and make it as smooth as possible.

'We'll need your shirt now, Iain,' he told his son for whom the sight of activity was having a palliative effect. Using the boy's shirt for binding he splinted the leg firmly to the branch. Ruth murmured slightly as he carried her to the entrance to the tunnel and laid her on the ground.

'I'll crawl backwards and take her shoulders. You take the tail of my shirt and keep her feet off the ground. Try not to jerk her leg if you can help it.' The boy nodded without speaking.

Even careful as they were, Ruth gave several small squeals of pain as they edged her along. Iain was able to keep below the level of the thorns, but the blood was running from his father's shoulders as they emerged. Despite her reaction in the tunnel, Ruth still had her eyes closed as they laid her down to allow themselves to rest.

'You run ahead,' Samuel instructed his son once they had recovered their breath.

'Tell your mother that Ruth has a broken leg and will need to get to hospital, Tell her to send somebody for Boss Roddy and tell him to bring his truck. I'll carry her home from here. Hurry now.'

Samuel was relieved that he was through the scrub and on the clear ground close to the huts before Ruth opened her eyes. At first she didn't focus properly then she spoke when she recognised the face above her.

'I'm sorry, Daddy.' Then she said, 'My leg's sore.'

'I know, but just be brave for a minute or two longer. We're almost home,' her father answered softly. Samuel entered his hut to find Naomi and Rebecca, the old woman who had attended the birth of both his children. A heavy blanket and pillow had been laid on the table and he eased his daughter gently down. Naomi gasped when she saw the sickening angle of the leg, but the older woman untied the wrapping shirt with a steady hand and made a close inspection.

Without comment she disappeared towards her own hut to appear back carrying a goat skin and a heavy knife with a slight curve in the blade. Nodding to Samuel to ease the broken leg off the table she slid the skin underneath. Using the knife which was razor sharp, she then cut slits in the skin so that it would be wrapped comfortably round the leg and bound it in place with strips of cloth which Naomi had produced. As she was completing the job by fixing the original splint they heard the tinny sound of an engine being pushed to its limit and Roddy MacLean appeared.

Calmly he walked to the table and smiled down at the wide eyed, ebony face.

'Weel, young lady, I know that you always said that you wanted me to take you to the city, but this is blackmail.' Then he turned to the parents. 'Fiona was tucking young Iain in with our two when I left. I've been putting off a visit to my lawyer and banker for far too long. We can easily stay a couple of nights and make up for the sleep we won't get tonight.'

'But we can never afford Nairobi hospital,' Naomi protested.

The big Scot smiled through several days growth of beard. 'There will be no need for money, the surgeon there is my mother's younger brother. He's only ten years older than me, the result, I believe, of bad weather and good whisky on a Hogmanay night when his parents mistakenly believed that they were beyond being affected by such things. His wife's a wee pet although she does come from Islay,' he added.

The journey over dirt roads was difficult for Ruth and a nightmare for her parents. Roddy had spread a layer of alfalfa hay on the floor of the truck and covered it with sacking. This cushioned the worst of the bumps but it was difficult to balance comfort with the need for haste. As they neared the city the road became smoother and Ruth slept. The first rays of the sun were lightening the eastern sky as they encountered the first houses of the rapidly expanding city. They hadn't seen another vehicle throughout the night.

'We'll go to his house first,' Roddy said over his shoulder. 'It'll save time in the end and the hospital is less than five minutes from there.'

Minutes later they drew up in front of a neat bungalow with a large well-kept garden. A light coloured car lay under an open sided lean-to at the side.

To Roddy's surprise, the door opened almost immediately to his sharp knock and revealed a short, chubby man with a shiny look of the neatly washed and shaved. He was wearing a white shirt and light shorts and had the type of legs which somehow surprised by the fact that they reached the ground.

A plump and very pretty woman appeared behind him and placed a hand on his shoulder, but before she could speak her husband gave a good-natured roar.

'Roddy Mhor, what on earth brings you here at a time when you used to be going to bed?'

'Well, Lachie, I would like to say that it was only the thought of one of Kate's breakfasts, but it's a bit more than that,' said Roddy and he explained in a couple of short sentences.

'I'll get a quick breakfast ready, Lachie,' said Kate as her husband moved forward first to reach and shake hands with the parents and then to look into the open eyes of their daughter.

'Well, young lady,' he smiled, 'what have you been doing to yourself?'

'I was running away from home,' she said to his astonishment.

Long afterwards, and even young as she then was, Ruth could remember her sense of wonder as she was carried into the hospital. After the two roomed hut which was her home the twelve bed ward seemed huge. Everything being painted a shining white increased the sense of space.

When she was settled on a bed, the surgeon sat facing her on the edge of it and took her wrist to check her pulse.

'Your knees are fat,' she said to the horror of her parents, but both Lachie and his nephew burst into laughter.

'That's because I always eat my porridge,' said the former. 'Now young lady,' he continued, 'I think that we should chase these folk out of the road so that you and I can get on with the job.'

'Can I sleep here tonight?' she asked.

'If you are good you can sleep here for a few nights,' replied a surprised Lachie.

'Then I'll be ever so good. This is a lovely big bed. Can Iain come too?'

Ruth was three months farther into her life by the time she left hospital. The selective memory of a child blocked out the spell of post-operative pain which the limited sedation of the time was unable to quell. What was firmly implanted was the kindness of the nurses and the cheerfulness of Lachie MacKinnon which seemed impervious to both exhaustion and disaster. Lachie's bubbly and rotund wee wife Kate brought in treats of home baking and sat on the edge of the bed to read stories to her.

The frequency of parents' visits was partly dictated by the availability of Roddy's truck. They were relieved if slightly miffed by the fact that their daughter had settled so well and didn't fret to get home with them whenever they were leaving her. The only time that this became a tearful occasion was when she was at the stage of being allowed out of bed and they brought Iain with them.

Morale was restored by Kate. 'Iain gets his school holidays soon and he can come and stay with us,' she said. 'Then he can come in and see you every day.'

This arrangement worked well for the MacLeod children and although Ruth still wasn't ready to go home by the time that Iain had to go back to school his sister accepted his departure with dry if rather bright eyes. The problem was in the MacKinnon household.

That evening Lachie entered his front door to the sound of his wife sobbing in their bedroom. This was something which he had feared. During the past few weeks he had watched his wife and the curly headed wee black boy going around hand-in-hand and a lump had formed in his own throat at the thought that she would never be able to do that with children of her own.

As he sat on the bed beside her she turned and buried her face in his shoulder. After a time her sobbing eased and her breathing returned to normal.

'I'm sorry, Lachie,' she said. 'I thought that I would have had all that over before you came in. I'll be all right now. It was just that the house seemed so quiet. Heavens your tea isn't ready' and she dashed off to the kitchen.

When first they had learned that Kate would never be able to bear a child they had discussed adoption, but in the end had decided against it. If they remained in Kenya a white child would have to go back to Britain for further education and they felt that it wouldn't be right to adopt a black child and then have to take it back to Britain if they decided to return. Both of them had accepted the situation and they had slipped into a very comfortable lifestyle, but the brightness and obvious intelligence of the MacLeod children had allowed all the old longing to resurface.

For the next couple of weeks Kate visited the hospital every day and took Ruth for walks in the grounds. Then came the day when her parents and brother arrived to take her home.

'We cannot thank you enough,' the tall black MacLeod told the two white MacKinnons as he gathered his daughter in his arms when she ran to him. 'When first I saw how bad the break was I never thought that I would see her run again.'

'To see her run like that gives us almost as much pleasure as it gives you,' Lachie assured him and went on, 'but if you feel yourself in our debt we can be easily repaid. Just bring your children through to stay with us as often as you can. I really cannot tell you how much we are going to miss them.'

Samuel bowed gravely. 'It will be a pleasure. No child can have too many parents,' he said looking at the delighted Kate.

At a nod from his mother, little Iain stepped forward and

shook hands with Lachie.

'Thank you for looking after my sister,' he said gravely. He then turned to shake hands with Kate, but as she leant forward he changed his mind and ran to throw his arms around her neck.

'I'll come to see you often,' he promised.

When Ruth went to school the MacKinnons took as much pleasure from the blossoming of her learning as did her own parents. Although Samuel and Naomi had never been educated beyond an advanced primary school level they were both intelligent people and it was obvious that this had transmitted itself to their children. Samuel was a natural linguist and his command of English was excellent. This gave Iain and Ruth an advantage over most of the other children who had only heard the Nilotic language of the Masai. Lachie and Kate who were both native Gaelic speakers were intrigued to learn that Samuel had a knowledge of Gaelic and liked to use this language when he came to drop off or pick up their welcome visitors.

When both Samuel and Naomi came to pick up their children after a two week stay, Lachie broached the subject of further education. Iain was approaching eleven years of age and had obviously reached the stage where he had outlived the mission school of his home village. It was Samuel who after a glance at his wife answered the question.

'This has been giving us thought for some time,' he said. 'For the time into which we were born, Naomi and I were fortunate from our misfortunes. Seonair and Grannie MacLeod gave us a chance in life which we never would have had by staying with our own people. Therefore Iain and Ruth are starting their climb of the ladder of life from a point several rungs higher than might otherwise have been the case. We would like this to continue but, of course, the governing factor is money. We simply cannot afford the cost involved in sending our children to Nairobi,' he ended the longest speech that the MacKinnons had ever heard him make.

Lachie and Kate were silent for a time before the latter

continued the conversation.

'Your children have brought something to our lives that we thought we could never have,' she said. 'We don't want, indeed I don't think we could bear to lose them. If you and Naomi agreed we would like to have Iain stay with us and attend school from here.'

'But we couldn't impose that on you,' Naomi protested. 'He isn't always as well behaved as he is when he is with you.'

'He's a boy and I was once one myself,' Lachie broke in, 'and when Ruth reaches that age we would like her to come too. Believe me, our motives are more selfish than they are altruistic. You can have no idea how much we miss them when they go away. Besides, Kate was a school teacher before we married and she can help with homework. She often complains that she is allowing her brain to stagnate. Think it over, but we would really like to have Iain as soon as it can be arranged and have them both when the time comes.'

Samuel looked at his wife who gave a slight nod before her face erupted into a wide, white toothed smile. Kate felt her own breath leave her body as the big, black man gave the answer she so desperately wanted to hear.

'We have no need of either discussion or further thought on this. Not only are you doing us a great favour but you have absolved us of a worry which has been with us for some time. There is only one condition. If either of the children ever misbehaves or questions your authority to discipline them you must let us know immediately. It is not good for the cockerel to be allowed to crow before his tail feathers have grown.'

Then his expression softened to mirror that of his wife. 'Now,' he continued, with a glance at Naomi, 'I think that we should inform our loin fruits of their good fortune.'

Iain, who was the more serious and introvert of the pair received the news with a joyous whoop but the normally ebullient Ruth took it with a serious face. For the next few weeks she joined in the general excitement of preparation for Iain's departure but after the event she retreated into an invisible shell. Several times in the following weeks her parents awoke to the sounds of her sobbing, but by the morning after she appeared to be quite bright as she went off to school.

When Naomi began to see Ruth's enthusiasm for her lessons beginning to wane she realised that there was more troubling her daughter than the want of her brother. It was Roddy MacLean who visited one day during school time and brought news of the likely cause of the malaise.

'Some of the older children, particularly the boys, have been giving her a hard time,' he told her mother. 'They are jealous of Iain going off to a big school in Nairobi and living in a house with white people. At first they started with just a bit of teasing, but as often happens when bullies are getting away with something it began to turn nasty.'

'What are we to do?' asked Naomi.

Roddy smiled. 'What needed to be done has already been seen to,' he said. 'The ringleader was the son of one of my best men. He is a big lump of a laddie and yesterday afternoon Jomo found him leading a group of miniature thugs who were harassing Ruth. Only once before have I seen Jomo in a rage and that was when he caught one of the other men lashing a young half broken colt with a bull-hide whip. The man was a fairly tough specimen but he wasn't fit to work for more than a week afterwards.

'Yesterday he herded the gang, which included some girls, into a corner. He then upended his own son and made the rest watch while he administered justice. Today he has taken the morning off work and gone to school for the first time in his life. Like many people with little or no education it annoys him to see people abusing the privilege.

'He has gone to make sure that his boy apologises to Ruth and to the rest of the school. It appears that unknown to the teachers this lad had been doing quite a bit of bullying. This may be the making of him. His gang will now see him from a different angle. One thing is sure is that he won't dare to bother Ruth again.'

His prediction proved correct. A few days afterwards the boy repeated his apology on a one-to-one basis and they became quite good friends. About a month later, on her ninth birthday, he presented her with a charcoal drawing of a fully extended running lion.

Many years later they were to meet by chance in Nairobi and she learned the root of his problems.

Because he had preferred drawing to other more boyish sports the other boys had taken to teasing him and calling him a cissy. This had caused him to fight back and in turn, when he discovered he could buy power with his fists, had led to bullying. By the time of their later meeting he was apprenticed to a firm of architects.

CHAPTER 3

By the time Iain had a couple of years in Nairobi behind him, Ruth was beginning to find her school work boring to the point of irritation. Time and again she hinted to her parents that she should now be allowed to join her brother. Samuel could maybe have been persuaded to agree but Naomi was unshakeable in her opinion that it was too soon to allow such a move.

'We are lucky,' she told her husband. 'We have found a home before we were old enough to realise that we didn't have one. Our children have a home. They are going to move out to a world of which, but for Seonair and Grannie, we would not have known. This is right and I am proud that they have the ability to do so. But we must make sure that they remember that this is their home and Kenya their country. Besides, we must not take over advantage of the good nature of Lachie and Kate.'

Naomi maintained her stance for another year before being forced to abandon the unequal fight. She very quickly found that their fear over abuse of the MacKinnon's hospitality was without foundation.

'We have been meaning to talk to you for some time,' confessed Lachie. 'First of all we will be delighted to have Ruth but we also wanted to talk about Iain. At first he talked about being a doctor, but I took him to the hospital a few times and he isn't too keen on the sight of blood. This would probably pass as he got more used to it, but it seems to have put him off the idea.

'However, on one of his visits he got talking to a patient of mine who is a lawyer. This man was very impressed with him and asked me to approach you with a view to Iain being taken on by his firm as a legal apprentice. I haven't said too much to Iain until I had spoken to you but I think that he would be keen on the idea. Don't think that this man is being charitable. He isn't. He is finding that more black people are coming to him with their problems and many of them would feel more comfortable speaking to a black man.'

After a glance at his wife, Samuel answered for both of them. 'We must leave the final decision to Iain, but it seems too good an opportunity to miss.'

Iain was enthusiastic, but his headmaster produced a temporary obstacle. First of all he spoke to Lachie and Kate, then one weekend travelled with his wife out to see Samuel and Naomi. 'I came to see you because I was afraid that you might not fully appreciate the career potential of your son,' he told Iain's parents. 'He is probably the brightest child that we have had at the school. I feel he would benefit greatly from another year of full time education with us. If he then wishes to pursue a career in law I would be pleased to take him for extracurricular lessons in the evenings.'

Seeing the beginning of doubt in the features of his listeners he hurriedly went on. 'I have already taken the liberty of speaking to Iain. It is the ambition of every child of his age to leave school as quickly as possible. But this is a gifted child with the ability to appreciate the future benefits of hard work.'

'But this would be putting you to tremendous trouble which we could never possibly repay,' Samuel protested.

The teacher was a tall, rather serious man but his face broke into the smile of one who sensed an argument won. 'But you must allow us to repay our debt,' he said as he reached to place a hand on the shoulder of his wife. 'We owe the life of our daughter to Dr MacKinnon. He could not be more proud of your children than if they were his own. Entirely apart from the sheer pleasure of teaching an able mind, I would like to do this for both him and his wife.'

Samuel and Naomi moved close to one another before the latter answered for both of them. 'At the moment we can do little but say how grateful we are to you. Perhaps some day we may be given the chance to do more.'

Despite her enthusiasm for the move, Ruth missed her parents badly on her first few weeks away from home. Kate, who had taught in areas of Scotland where the children from the glens had to move into lodgings in the towns if they wanted secondary education, recognised the familiar symptoms. Previous visits had the brevity and excitement of holiday mood to carry her through but this was a permanent landing on the stairway of adult life. After consultation with Kate, Iain's headmaster had set him a fairly exacting syllabus so that he had little time to spend on the entertainment of his homesick sister.

One Saturday afternoon at the end of her first month with them, Kate suggested to Ruth that she walk towards the hospital to meet Lachie who should soon be on his way home. After a few very hot days the temperature had eased a little and Ruth, who already promised to be tall like her father, found it pleasant to walk past the gardens of the ever growing suburbs of Nairobi toward the hospital.

As she approached the entrance door Lachie appeared but before they could greet one another Ruth was just aware of a scuffling sound behind her before a blow on her shoulder knocked her sideways. She recovered her balance just in time to see Lachie snatch a child from the arms of a young black woman before the woman collapsed at his feet.

As he hesitated looking for a place to put down the baby, Ruth ran forward.

'Give the baby to me. You attend to the mother,' she commanded so positively that he instantly obeyed and knelt to grasp the wrist of the woman who was breathing with a heavy rasping sound. After a moment he rose saying, 'I think that she's just exhausted. I'll get somebody with a stretcher,' before the shocked eyes of Ruth silenced him. Then he became aware of a faint buzzing sound and a sweet sickening smell.

A glance at the olive face of a well nourished girl of about two years of age supplied the reason. On the left cheek was a horrible suppurating wound which was covered in flies. As

Lachie leaned forward for a closer look the eyes of the child opened, focused and widened in terror at the sight of his face and a faint squeak escaped from among the buzzing swarm which surrounded her mouth. Ruth turned the baby to cuddle her and as her face came into line of sight the small tensed body relaxed.

'That looks like a bite, probably from a dog,' Lachie told Ruth. 'Can you cope until I get people to help the mother? Take the baby to my office first until we dispose of these flies and get a better look.'

Lachie got back to his office to find Ruth sitting in the chair behind his desk. Her lithe young body was moving back and forth in a gentle rocking motion. The baby was staring wide-eyed into her face and she was crooning softly. The exiled doctor swallowed a sudden lump in his throat when he recognised the tune of 'Over the Sea to Skye.'

As he moved into its line of vision the child gave a high-pitched animal squeal of terror and tried to hide against Ruth's chest. Motioning Lachie to step back she cuddled the little girl for a moment or two then, when it was again relaxed, she sat the baby facing her on her knees and began to speak softly in the Nilotic clicking language of the Masai. The smell from the wound and the noise from the unwelcome attenders seemed to permeate every corner of the clinically white room. Still speaking softly in the same language Ruth, reaching out her left hand, took Lachie by the right hand and drew him round to behind her shoulder from where he could see the wound in his patient. After a moment and without a pause in the sound of her voice she moved his hand up to press against her own cheek then eased it forward to the right cheek of the baby. Momentarily, the small body tensed then as Ruth stopped speaking to smile she found her smile returned.

'We'll have to get rid of these flies first,' said Lachie softly. 'I'll bring a nurse back with me.'

Lachie came back escorting a black nurse who was pushing a trolley. Lachie heard a sharp intake of breath from the nurse at the sight of the baby but made no comment. Taking a white muslin he soaked it in a liquid, came round to where the baby could see him clearly, paused for a moment then gently laid it over the mass on the small cheek. After a moment he folded the corners inward and lifted off the cloth.

'This isn't as bad as I thought,' he said after a closer inspection then he leaned forward to sniff. 'There is a smell from the wound but I think that there's another source as well.'

'I know,' smiled Ruth. 'I can feel a dampness on my knees. I'll be a bit unsocial when I stand up.'

'Can you hold on until we get this end sorted? I don't want to stop while we appear to be winning the battle of confidence.'

'Of course,' then she leaned forward to bury her face in the baby's stomach and waggled her head. 'Who's a stinky wee thing,' she said in English. The baby laughed.

When the professional job was done Ruth carried the baby through to the sluice room and held her while the nurse attended to the practicalities. Then when daughter and anxious mother were reunited in the ward and Ruth had gone to clean herself up, Lachie called the nurse into his office.

'Do you know that mother and baby?' he asked when the girl was seated.

'Can you tell me the story?' he added after a nod. There was a pause, another nod and the nurse began to speak. The mother's parents lived and worked on a farm which was about ten miles from the city. A bright child, she had caught the eye of a missionary who had arranged for her to be educated in a school run by Roman Catholic nuns. The nurse had attended the same school where she remembered the mother being one of the older girls.

On leaving school she had taught young children in the school which served the village in which the nurse had been born and where her parents still lived. When the mother of the young teacher died suddenly she had left the school to go home to look after her father.

'It was terrible,' said the nurse. 'The children were crying. They didn't want her to go but she had to obey her father.'

At first she had combined the care of her father with teaching in another small school, but the farmer had an over-indulged son and the two became friendly.

'She was foolish. The man was not good.'

When the farmer learned she was pregnant by his son he was furious and tried to make her have an abortion. When she refused, he sent his son to a new life in Canada although the boy didn't appear to want the baby any more than his father did. Her own father had died a few months previously.

'Since then the farmer has made life bad for her.' The girl went on. 'He wants to drive her away. He has fierce dogs. It would be one of them which bit the baby and he wouldn't care.' There was a pause, then 'Can we keep her here? She would be a good nurse and they could share my room.'

'I'll talk to her,' promised Lachie. 'She may not want that but we cannot let her go back to where she and her baby are going to be at risk. What you have told me explains the fact that the baby is terrified of a white man. If Ruth hadn't been here we would have had to sedate her. Now I'd better find that girl and get her home. Kate will be thinking that we're lost.'

He found Ruth sitting by the bed nursing the chortling baby and talking to its mother.

As they walked home she slipped her hand into his.

'Uncle Lachie, I want to be a doctor,' she said.

CHAPTER 4

'I hope that she sticks to the idea,' Lachie told Kate later that evening as he recounted the tale. 'Neither the wound nor the general unpleasantness seemed to bother her. Without her the baby would have been terrified.'

Any doubts that he had were groundless. Ruth had inherited the tenacity of her father and this combined with the native African tolerance of repetition meant that any goal which she set herself would eventually be reached. Her thirst for knowledge meant that study was more pleasure than chore and this was greatly helped by the facilities that the MacKinnons were able to provide. Not the least of these was an extensive and relevant library of books and the privacy of her own room was invaluable. Here, when tiredness overcame diligence, she often sat to dream of what might lie hidden in her future. She was under no illusion concerning the goals which Iain and she had set for themselves.

If they were successful the transformation from jungle hut to professional life would be immense. And although she tried to keep it hidden in her mind she was at times uneasy about moving into a world where the predominant skin colour would be opposite to her own.

She made no really close friends but she was generally popular with her classmates although many of them would have liked to have had her brain. One boy, the son of a wealthy white business man was more jealous than the rest and did all that he could to make life miserable for her. Being a natural bully he had kept quiet while her big brother was still at school but when Iain left he began a merciless campaign of harassment.

A black girl from an impecunious family who was living as a white in an expensive area of the city made him think that he had ready-made ammunition to hand and he never missed an opportunity to belittle her. For a long time Ruth maintained her dignity, but one particularly cruel taunt provoked her to the extent that she was finally forced into retaliation. He had left a bunch of bananas on her desk with an attached label on which he had written 'The food of your ancestors'. Previously he had been content with snide remarks but as Ruth moved to her desk before the teacher came into the classroom she was aware that the rest of the class was waiting for her reaction. In the midst of a silence she picked up the bunch and moved across the room to place them on his desk in front of the boy.

'When my ancestors were chieftains in the Rift Valley yours were grubbing for roots in an Irish bog,' she told him. The boy blushed crimson with rage as the rest of the class laughed. His father, who had made good in Kenya mainly because of hard work, was Irish and proud of it, but his mother was snooty middle class English who thought that she had married down market.

On marriage she had made her husband drop the prefix O' from his name and hyphenated her own name to his in its place. Both she and her son cultivated a three dimensional accent which they hoped sounded upper class English and scorned Hybernianism of any kind. In the eyes of the boy, Ruth could not have chosen a greater insult and he muttered under his breath as she went back to her seat.

As the class broke up in the afternoon, Ruth spent some time putting together homework and the other pupils had all left as she stepped outside the gate to find the boy waiting. She stopped in alarm but he stepped forward smiling and holding out his hand.

'Okay, you win, let's be friends,' he said.

Ruth was only too happy to put the whole tiresome business behind her and as their routes home coincided for part of the way she made no objection when he fell into step beside her. For a time they chatted pleasantly as they strolled past neat gardens in many of which black men were working, but then they came to an area with bush on either side of the road and no houses in sight. Suddenly the boy lunged his shoulder into her ribs knocking her off balance and followed up the attack by pushing her backwards off the road through a gap in the scrub.

Ruth was a strong girl but the ferocity of the attack took her completely by surprise. Her books flew from her hands. As she was forced farther from the road her heel caught on a stone and she crashed to the ground. Her skirt rucked up around her waist exposing her long smooth legs and white pants. The force of the fall had winded Ruth and as she lay gathering her senses the boy straightened, fumbled for a time with shaking hands at his belt, then pushing his trousers to his ankles he dropped to his knees beside her. Choosing her moment she bent up her legs and smashed her feet into his rib cage forcing all the air out of his lungs. Getting quickly to her feet she completed the removal of his trousers, turned him on his face and knelt on his back as she used the light cotton to securely tie his hands behind him.

As she picked up his belt with the intention of tying his feet she heard a girl's voice scream, 'There's her books,' and two girls and two boys, all from her class at school, burst through the bush towards her.

'Are you all right?' one of the girls asked Ruth as the four ran forward. Then she saw the red faced and bare bottomed Cecil Barclay-Brian struggling to free his hands and burst into peals of laughter which quickly found an echo from her companions. The two boys stepped to either side of him and hauled him to his feet where he presented an even sorrier spectacle. A string of oaths which began to issue from his lips was suddenly cut by the expression on the faces of the boys. One of them picked up the belt, stepped behind him and cracked it across plump buttocks before Ruth caught his arm.

'No,' she said, 'just untie his hands and let him go.'

'Och, naw,' said the other boy who was the carbon copy of a red haired Scotsman, 'we canna hae a Sassenach thinkin' he can get away wi' abusin' a lassie. We'll juist take him hame as he is. His mammie can untie his hands.'

Despite Ruth's protests her tormentor was pushed out into the open and made to precede them along the road. By this time his tantrum was replaced by tears of self pity, but with the belt occasionally swishing close enough to his nether regions for him to feel its draught he was forced to keep walking. As they came into sight of houses Ruth suddenly grabbed the belt and ran round in front to bring the procession to a halt.

'This has gone far enough,' she said forcibly. Then, ignoring the blubbering boy, she addressed her friends.

'Let him go. It would have been different if he had succeeded but he didn't and I don't think that he'll be keen on his friends finding out that he was beaten by a wee black girl.'

After a pause the red haired boy spun Barclay-Brian round by the shoulder and spoke into his face.

'Right, we'll let ye go,' he said. 'But mind it's Ruth that's lettin' ye go an' no' us an' if she reports ye tae the heidie we'll back her up.'

At his nod the other boy unknotted the trousers and handed them to their owner.

'Are you going to report him? You should,' said one of the girls as Ruth thanked her rescuers.

'No, I'd rather it was all forgotten. What made you come after me?'

'We heard him boasting to that wee rat, Howard, about what he was going to do. We ran after Alastair and George and got them to come back with us. They didn't think that he meant it but we did. He's a creep.'

Cecil Barclay-Brian was absent from school on the following day, but appeared just before the bell on the day after. He never approached Ruth and all of that day she worried that he would again accost her in the afternoon.

But as she emerged between the entrance pillars it was to see Roddy MacLean's truck waiting for her.

Ruth could detect anxiety behind the smile of the big,

rough white man as she climbed into the hot cab beside him.

'Your mother isn't well, Ruth,' he said in answer to her question. 'She had been sick before your father got home yesterday. She seemed to be alright for a while, but then she was sick again and began to get a bit of pain. Your father came for me just after three this morning. We waited until after sun up but when she seemed to be getting more pain we took her to Lachie at the hospital.'

'She's very ill, isn't she?'

There was a slight pause then, 'If it wasn't for Lachie Beag I would be really worried, but if there's anybody can help her he's the man. I would rather see her here being looked after by him than in the biggest hospital in London.'

'How's Dad?' she asked as he started the engine.

'Och, that man's needing a skelp. He's killing himself trying to look after other folk. He was exhausted when he arrived home last night and now he's had a night without sleep. Kate was pouring malt whisky into him when I left.'

When they reached the house, Ruth could all too clearly see the reason for Roddy's anger. Her father's normally smooth black features were grey and lined. She ran forward to drop to her knees beside him and his arm encircled her shoulders. After a time she leant back to look into his face. Neither spoke as she again buried her face in his chest. All the tensions of the previous four days exploded as one and sobs racked her young frame.

After a time Kate's hands on her shoulders drew Ruth to her feet. 'Get changed before we have something to eat,' ordered the older woman, 'then we can go to the hospital.'

Roddy and Kate waited outside while father and daughter went to Naomi's bedside. After a moment or two Lachie joined them from another part of the hospital.

'I am not too happy,' he said in answer to Roddy's question. 'Black women in my experience have a fairly high pain threshold and are expert in the practice of stoicism, but Naomi is showing a lot of signs of discomfort.'

'What do you suspect?' asked his wife then, when he

hesitated, she pressed further. 'Come on, Lachie, I know you too well. There's something going on in that head of yours.'

Instead of answering, her husband turned to Roddy.

'Tell me,' he asked, 'has there been any form of family crisis or has Samuel been away from home for any longer than the usual period a few weeks ago?'

'Well, yes,' came the answer after a moment of thought, 'as grazing land has become scarcer so some of the tribal disputes have become nastier. Just before the rains came and the grass started to grow Samuel was called away to mediate in one where a couple of men had been killed. We were to look after his cattle for a couple of days but the rains came and he couldn't get home for more than a week. I'll tell you that I was damned glad to see him when he finally turned up. I knew that he would take risks in order to get home and I was afraid that he could be swept away trying to cross a river.'

The eyes of the other two turned to the surgeon who was silent for a time. 'Useful,' he said softly 'that could explain it.'

'Well,' Kate put the single word in the form of a question.

'It had to be some form of ectopia,' then his anxious expression relaxed into what was almost a smile, 'but this now looks like being man made. We can deal with that. Only I'll have to operate right away.'

'Lachie, you can't,' Kate burst out. 'You have to sleep. This would be two nights with no rest.'

'I must,' he said firmly. 'If I don't, Ruth will be left with only one mother.' Then the humour which was forever close to the surface shone through his obvious anxiety.

'Just you warm the bed and I'll be there before the night's through and I might even sleep for a while,' he added mischievously before kissing her deeply and turning to hurry away.

'I'm glad that he's just my uncle and not my father,' said Roddy, 'I couldn't cope with a wee brother or sister at my age.' But he wished that he could have recaptured the escaped words when he saw a tear roll through the smile on Kate's face.

Lachie persuaded Samuel and Ruth to go back to the house with Roddy and Kate. Ruth went to bed, where Kate brought her a hot drink but despite his obvious weariness Samuel wanted to sit up until Lachie came home. However, with inherited Hebridean wisdom, Kate prescribed and administered a generous malt whisky and he had barely finished this when his big head began to nod.

In the early hours of the morning Kate felt Lachie creep into bed beside her.

'Ectopic pregnancy,' he said in answer to her murmured question. 'There's a bit of inflammation but Fleming's new drug should deal with that.'

'Most surprise pregnancies occur either after a period of separation or just after some family triumph or crisis,' Lachie told the sheepish but relieved Samuel and Naomi the next day. The hangdog expression on the face of her husband made Naomi start a laugh which was turned into a grimace of pain by the drag of her stitches.

'At our age we should have known better,' she said when she got her breath back, 'but for a few days I thought that he was providing a meal for a litter of lion cubs,' she ended as she reached for the big competent hand of her mentor.

CHAPTER 5

The day before his mother was to be released from hospital Iain arrived back in Nairobi. He had spent almost a month at Thika where his firm had a branch. After a quick call at the office he hurried excitedly to see his mother. His firm wanted to send him to university in London to take his Bachelor of Law degree. Iain had always been practical and as he matter-of-factly explained that all costs were being met by his employers, Naomi was more excited than her son.

Despite her obvious and expressed yearning to get home it was another fortnight before Lachie would allow Naomi to make the journey. The last part was over dirt roads which he knew would still be feeling the effects of the rains.

'If you were going to be sitting on the back of a sensible Highland pony I might let you go,' he told her, 'but you are going to be driven by Roddy Mor and he took his driving lessons from Jehu.'

For the first time in her life she found what it was like to be spoiled. Samuel and Naomi worried that they would never be able to repay Lachie and Kate for what they were doing for their children but the latter pair felt that they owed a debt to the former for unselfishly sharing their talented children. So despite the fact that Samuel was an exceptionally considerate husband whose first thoughts were always for his family, neither his facilities nor his means could have provided the luxury which his wife enjoyed during her convalescence.

Iain's firm gave him two weeks leave before he left for London and as this coincided with part of Ruth's school holiday the MacLeod family were able to share one roof for what was a very happy time.

Ruth returned from that holiday to a time of intense study. Several firms and some wealthy individuals were offering scholarships to enable students to continue their studies in European universities. With a view to taking advantage of this facility the school had revised their curriculum and taken on some highly qualified and enthusiastic teachers which in turn put pressure on the pupils. As Ruth had never wavered in her intention to be a doctor she spent as much time as possible at the hospital with Lachie, who took extreme pride in his protégée and never tired of explaining things to her. The pair were a familiar sight in the wards at all times of the day and night,.

Kate missed Iain badly at first, but she was more content when letters started to arrive telling that he was enjoying London. Although Kate had gone to university in Glasgow and worked there for a time before her marriage she had a slight fear of cities and had never felt really comfortable when hemmed in by people and buildings. Despite the fact that Nairobi seemed to be growing daily there was a feeling of vast empty spaces about Kenya which pleased her.

She had never found it easy to persuade Lachie to take time off but purchase of an ex-army jeep had rediscovered the wee boy who had always lurked in his nature. They both loved watching the wild animals and birds in which the country abounded and although sometimes a bit frightened in the places to which he took her in his new-found toy Kate was too pleased to see her husband relaxed to offer protest. However, this was a vehicle which had seen some service and much abuse in the North African war and even to Kate's unskilled ears the engine sounded noisy. From her childhood and youth she had memories of many unreliable cars and worried about the possible consequences of a breakdown in a remote area. Now he had announced that if she stocked up with provisions they would take a week and venture farther afield.

'Ruth is quite capable of looking after herself and now that you haven't got Iain to mollycoddle we don't need to hurry back,' he teased.

Kate sang softly as she worked. The MacLeod children had

completely changed life for Lachie and herself. Being West Coast of Scotland fatalists they never questioned the good fortune which had blended the lives of the two families but they were nonetheless grateful. On many occasions she had suffered depression from the knowledge that she would never have children of her own. Then she had found a ready made pair whose unselfish parents didn't mind sharing them. She smiled at the thought that some day she would take them to her home island and introduce them to the more staid of her elderly relatives.

Before Iain had gone off to London she had stood him against a wall in his bare feet while she herself stood on a chair to measure his height. He was just over six feet with the broad shoulders of his father and the patrician features which betrayed the Moorish ancestry of both of his natural parents. A son to be proud of. She jumped when she felt two hands on her shoulders. Turning, she looked into the laughing face of her husband with the taller figure of Ruth smiling over his shoulder.

'You would think that somebody going on safari would be singing something with more of a spirit of adventure in it than "In Praise of Islay",' he teased. 'I've never seen any lions in Port Ellen except maybe on a Saturday night.

Ruth stepped round to give Kate a quick cuddle. 'Never you mind him, Aunt Kate,' she said, 'I'm quite sure that an Islay kelpie would see off a Kenya lion any day.'

'Och, yes,' Kate agreed, 'and the Skye kelpie was just a Shetland pony that got caught by the tide.'

Next morning they offered to drop Ruth off at the school on their road away but when she saw how little room was left on the loaded jeep she elected to walk. Kate had left a plentiful supply of tins along with a survival list of instructions which prompted Lachie to question how long she intended to be away.

'I know how much you can eat in a week, Lachie MacKinnon,' she told him, 'and Ruth can have some of her pals round to keep her company while we're away. We can't have them thinking that we left her to starve.'

For the first couple of nights Ruth used the solitude to good advantage to get on with study for impending exams. But both of the MacKinnons were ebullient characters and the house seemed empty without them. By the weekend when she had been four days on her own Ruth was glad of the company of the two girls who had rescued her from Cecil Barclay-Brian.

'They're due back here on Thursday,' Ruth said in answer to a question from one of the girls, 'but if Uncle Lachie can wait away from his patients for as long as that I'll be surprised.'

Ruth hurried home from school on the Wednesday afternoon fully expecting to see the jeep at the door but she was disappointed. On Thursday morning she rose early and tidied the whole house before she left. But she had to go to bed that night with no sign of the returning travellers. By Friday afternoon she was becoming concerned and made a fruitless check with the hospital.

Saturday still drew a blank and it was a seriously worried Ruth who eventually fell asleep after reading far into the night. Early on Sunday morning she awoke to the sound of a car. Grabbing a light dressing gown which had been a Christmas present from Lachie and Kate, she ran to open the door. But instead of the plump, smiling couple whom she had expected, she was met by the tall figures of Samuel and Roddy. Their expressions told her that something was seriously wrong and she ran to her father.

'What happened? Tell me,' she said urgently against his chest.

For a moment he held her in his arms, then, 'They are both death, Ruth,' he said quietly with a sob in his voice.

She heard a clock behind her chime five times before she collapsed in a dead faint.

Ruth woke up in bed with her father sitting nearby.

'There was a thunderstorm in the mountains and they were caught in a flash flood,' came the gentle explanation. 'A group of tribesmen saw it happen. They had just driven their cattle over the river which was only a trickle and Lachie and Kate waved to them as they met. But when the jeep was half way across it stalled with a front wheel against a rock. Then just as Lachie had succeeded in getting it started the flood caught them. It washed both of them out of their seats.

'The men heard the water just before it appeared but Lachie wouldn't have been able to hear above the engine noise. They were dashed against a rock and died instantly. I doubt if they even knew what happened.'

The bodies were brought back to Nairobi for burial. The jeep had been carried down the river and was smashed to pieces. The two coffins were lowered side by side into the dry red earth of the graves. A Scottish minister pronounced the words of committal in Gaelic. Samuel stood dry eyed and stern faced. He was conscious of a movement beside him and big Roddy MacLean, normally the most undemonstrative of men, placed an arm round his shoulders. The two men were of equal height and they stood there in a solid wall of silent sadness. As the last corner of shiny wood disappeared under the shovelled soil they turned away to be met by the senior partner of the law firm where Iain worked. He was a lean man, the second generation of an English family which had come to Kenya while Queen Victoria still reigned.

Solemnly he shook hands first with Roddy then with Samuel before making his request.

'Could you two gentlemen come to my office tomorrow morning?' At their nod he added, 'Shall we say around ten o'clock. Excellent, excellent.' Then he turned away.

When Roddy and Samuel got back to the MacKinnons' house they were surprised to find Ruth playing in the garden with a bonny wee brown skinned child. 'This is Sarah,' she told them. 'Her mother, Anna, is in the house. She's very upset.' Despite her romping with the child, Ruth's own eyes were glistening with unshed tears.

They reached the door to the sound of uncontrolled sobbing and inside found their two wives struggling to comfort a young black woman who was a stranger to them both. Fiona, Roddy's wife, rose to her feet and motioned the two men to follow her into the kitchen.

'That's the girl whose baby was bitten on the face by a dog,' she told them. 'Lachie had arranged accommodation for her and her daughter and she was training to be a nurse. He was also arranging for Sarah to go to school. Not only has she lost the only white man who has ever shown her kindness but she fears that she will lose everything else as well.'

'What can we do with her?' her husband asked.

'Just what Lachie and Kate would have done. We'll keep her here for tonight. All of us need sleep. Tomorrow is a day yet untouched. We must live with the living. We cannot live with the dead. But we must try to do as they would have wanted us to do,' she ended decisively.

As is the way with so many of life's problems, delay gave the solution time to emerge. Roddy and Samuel found themselves ushered into an office which was a throwback to the times of Charles Dickens. Even in the heat of a tropical morning the lawyer rose to greet them clad in a dark suit with his thin neck encased in a stiff winged collar and bow tie. When they were seated he shuffled some papers before dropping his glasses to the point of his nose to look over them at his visitors.

'Dr and Mrs MacKinnon came to see me a few months ago,' he said. 'They each made Wills in favour of the other, but in each Will there is incorporated a common calamity clause which now becomes relevant. Under that clause you gentlemen are joint executors of the combined estates. You have total discretion to administer the estates to what you consider to be the best advantage of the legatees.'

He looked at Samuel and a faint smile crossed his face. 'The sole beneficiaries of the estates are, and here I quote, "our dear adoptive children, Mr Iain MacLeod and Miss Ruth MacLeod who have done so much to enrich our lives".'

Samuel was silent for a moment then, 'But we can't do that,' he burst out, 'what about their other relations?'

He was stopped by Roddy's hand on his shoulder.

'Do you remember what Fiona said yesterday about what Lachie and Kate would have wanted?' At a nod of the grizzled head he went on, 'Well this is what they wanted, otherwise they wouldn't have done it. We owe it to them to see their wishes are carried out.'

The lawyer cleared his throat.

'Mr MacLeod,' he said, 'it is extremely irregular that I should comment but in this case I will make an exception for two reasons. My wife and myself were unable to have children.' The voice of the dignified old man broke almost to a sob before he went on. 'Because of this I can appreciate how fortunate Dr and Mrs MacKinnon considered themselves to be allowed to share in the lives of your children.

'Please do not misunderstand me, but in many cases the parents of intelligent children just do not appreciate the blessing which been bestowed on them. Your son, Iain, is the brightest young man who has ever passed through this office. You owe it to the memory of the MacKinnons to see that he has the chance to develop his potential to its fullest extent and his sister will become an excellent doctor.'

Again he paused as though surprised by his own temerity before ending.

'The assets are two life assurance policies which, because the deaths were resultant from an accident, will each pay slightly in excess of ten thousand pounds. There is also a cash balance which, after funeral expenses, will come to around two thousand pounds. Then, of course, there is the house which is free of encumbrance.'

On being given the news Naomi began to voice similar objections to those of her husband but was stopped by Fiona.

'You remember what I said yesterday?' At a nod from the tall black woman she went on after a rather defensive glance at her husband. 'Kate spoke to me about this the last time we were in Nairobi. She and Lachie were planning to ask you about sending Ruth to London for her medical training. Provided she continues to pass exams which I don't doubt for a minute, that could be in just over a year's time.'

She then turned to face the two men. 'Now I have a suggestion. Ruth is perfectly capable and she has a lot of good pals. But a young girl staying on her own can get lonely. Lachie seemed to think a lot of this girl, Anna. Her wee lassie, Sarah, is soon going to school. I think that you should let her move in here if Ruth is agreeable.'

Ruth accepted the suggestion with enthusiasm and on their next visit her parents were pleased to see that the arrangement was working well. Anna was a good cook and housekeeper and her bubbly daughter kept Ruth from dwelling too much on the circumstances which had brought them all under the one roof. Lachie's hospital was also doing its best to be helpful and Anna was able to continue her training during the time that Sarah was at school.

One evening when Ruth came home she noticed that the older girl was quieter than usual and appeared to have been crying. Normally, after playing with Sarah before she went to bed, Ruth went off to her room to study, but on this occasion she stayed to probe the reason for Anna's distress. When she put the question there was silence for a moment before the girl dissolved in floods of tears.

'Sarah's grandfather was admitted to the hospital yesterday afternoon,' she told Ruth. 'He has a wound in his thigh which he neglected and has developed septicaemia. I went to dress it today and he recognised me. While I was dressing the wound he was quiet, but when I was taping down the bandage he suddenly grabbed my hand and pulled it towards his groin.

'Oh, Ruth, he was horrible. When I screamed he started to shout that if I got into the bed he would show me that the father was a better man than the son and he would give me another little black bastard. I know I did wrong, but I loved his son and thought that he loved me. I have to go back to that ward tomorrow. What am I to do?'

'I wish Uncle Lachie was here,' said Ruth crossly. 'He wouldn't stand for this.'

When Anna arrived at the hospital on the following

morning, she was summoned to the office of the matron. This was a massively formidable lady from Aberdeenshire who had gone to Kenya at the end of the First World War and had never been back to Scotland since. She mothered all the staff. This had included Lachie and she was still having difficulty in accepting that he was no longer there.

'Why dinna ye tell me that Mr Howard gave ye trouble yesterday?' she demanded when the girl was seated. When Anna hesitated to reply, she went on in a softer tone, 'Listen, lass, there's naebody here that's gaun tae blame ye ower the heid o' a lecherous auld nyaff like thon. An' if he wis tae get awa' wi' it this time he wid juist dae it again wi' some o' the ither lassies an' Ah'm no' goin, tae huv that. Noo, Ah'm gaun tae plester his auld erse the day an' you're gaun tae help me. Get you the trolley ready an' Ah'll be wi' ye in a meenit.'

When they reached their patient he was sitting on the side of his bed dressed in shirt and trousers and he obviously didn't realise that the matron was also coming to him. There were two other patients in the ward but both had been operated on early that morning and still hadn't come out of anaesthetic and she could have been coming to check on them. He soon found that luck wasn't with him.

'Slip aff thae breeks, man, an' lie doon on the left,' he was brusquely ordered.

For a moment he hesitated and started to protest but the dominant look of the substantial white clad lady silenced him and he slowly complied. As he lay on his left side he cupped his hands round his groin.

'Ye made a good job o' that dressin' considerin' the circumstances,' Anna was told. 'Noo, lass, juist strip it off an' we'll hae a look at whit's below.'

As Anna carefully began to ease off the plaster the patient made small noises of pain which the matron chose to disregard.

'Och, lass, that's gaun tae tak far ower lang,' she told the nurse. 'Wait you an' Ah'll show ye a quicker wey.'

So saying, she stepped forward and took a firm grip of the

42

edge of the plaster with her right hand, then she raised her left hand and brought it down with a resounding slap on the bare buttock while ripping the plaster off with one quick flick of her right. The patient yelled and his hands jerked forward but again he was ignored. As he sought to cover his modesty the older woman glanced down before turning to the younger.

'Ye ken,' she said with a twinkle in her eye, 'when I wis a quinie Ah used tae fish for cuddies in the Don wi' a worm that was bigger than that.'

Wisely, the man on the bed made no comment.

CHAPTER 6

Despite some careful brainwashing which had been done by Lachie, Samuel and Naomi saw the approach of the end of Ruth's schooldays with mixed feelings. They were proud of the ability of their children and wished their daughter to repeat the success of their son but this meant that she would have to follow his footsteps to qualify in London.

From the moment of making her decision to study medicine, the main doubt in Ruth's mind had been the financial cost of the venture. She had been afraid to voice this to either Lachie or Kate lest they think that she was asking for help, but their legacy now meant that she owed it to their memory to do well. She knew that Iain had been homesick when he first went to London but as he made friends he began to enjoy the bustle of the city.

Anna and Sarah came to the airport to see her off. Sarah cried. Then take-off was delayed because of severe sand storms in Southern Sahara which were affecting visibility at Khartoum airport. The delay eventually extended to more than four hours, by which time tiredness was an added factor to the distress of the little girl and the final leave taking was hysterical. There was a further delay in take-off from Khartoum. Instead of landing in London on Friday afternoon an exhausted Ruth finally got there on Saturday morning.

Her eventual introduction to the capital of the Empire was marred by an ugly incident as she stepped off the airport bus. She was carrying a bag of hand luggage which caught on the step and caused her to stagger and she collided with a tubby, bowler-hatted gentleman knocking off his hat and almost causing him to fall.

'Black bitch', he said explosively as he gathered himself together. 'Why didn't you stay in the trees where you belong?'

Ruth was on the point of bursting into tears when a tall distinguished looking man stepped forward.

'My office, Monday morning, 9 o'clock,' he told the discomfited aggressor as he took the distressed girl by the elbow to turn her away.

'Since this is an airport bus I take it that you have just arrived in London,' said her champion as they walked towards the luggage which was being stacked on the ground. 'Is this your first visit?' he asked.

At her nod, he went on, 'Then don't give another thought to the character who has just departed. Now,' as he retrieved her case, 'would you like a cup of coffee as an apology by one Briton for the conduct of another?'

In the course of the next hour Ruth learned that the man was a senior civil servant. As a young man he had held a post in Nyasaland and there he had met his wife who was the daughter of a black woman and a white Scot who was farming there. The father had honoured his responsibilities and she had been sent to Britain to finish her education. They had married in London and had a son and a daughter but the boy had been killed as a fighter pilot in the Battle of Britain.

'We were so proud of him that I thought that his mother would never get over it,' he said with a catch in his voice, 'but our daughter was a nurse and she met a Scotsman who had been wounded on a commando raid. They have been married for four years and their son has just turned two. We just feel so lucky. Our son-in-law has just inherited the family estate in a lovely part of Argyll and when I retire we are going to look for a house near to them. Now, young lady,' he said as he rose to his feet, 'we'd better find you a taxi and stop boring you with the story of my life.'

He insisted on paying for the taxi and before closing the door he handed her his card.

'Get in touch with us once you get settled. My wife would love to meet you.'

The card gave an address in Richmond of Mr James Wright.

The next few weeks passed quickly for Ruth and the brief encounter slipped to the back of her mind. She was pleased to find that there were several black and coloured students from various parts of the world and her original fears of being an oddity disappeared.

Because of her upbringing in a close-knit village community Ruth had seen several dead people but in the hospital in Nairobi, Lachie had shielded her from such things. She was soon to learn that there was a vast difference between a neatly laid out corpse and a cadaver on a mortuary slab. On her first group visit two of the boys were sick. A girl called Jackie who was standing in front of Ruth began to sway in slow motion and Ruth just managed to grasp her before she collapsed in a faint. The mortuary staff had obviously seen such an event many times before and help was soon at hand.

'I feel such a fool,' the girl told Ruth when she recovered. 'I slept in this morning and missed out on breakfast. I won't do that again.'

The two became friends and when Jackie said that she lived in Richmond Ruth produced James Wright's calling card.

'Oh, yes, Mr Wright. He lives at the end of our road. Where did you meet him?'

Ruth told the story and the other girl went on.

'Yes, I can just remember their son in his RAF uniform. He used to take the boys to play football on Saturdays and my older brother was badly cut up when he died. Are you going to get in touch?'

'I don't know. I feel that I maybe just caught him at an emotional moment and don't like to bother them. What do you think?'

'I think that you should. I think that you would be good for Mrs Wright. Not only did she lose her son, but just near the end of the war one of her best friends was killed by a flying bomb. Why don't you come home with me next weekend and we'll both visit?'

'Are you sure that will be alright with your parents, Jackie?'

'Worry not. Mum welcomes everybody. Even the stray

cats come to our door. And my dad and brother will love you.' Then she laughed, 'It will be interesting to see your effect on the old man's blood pressure.'

Ruth found that Jackie had not exaggerated the scale of the welcome which she would receive. Mr and Mrs Murray introduced themselves as Hugo and Joyce. Hugo was a handsome man now showing some signs of the battle against rotundity of the slowed-down sportsman. Joyce had the chubby cheeked prettiness of someone who had never been slim and had long since accepted the situation. George, their son, had the broad shoulders of a rugby player and the used paper bag features of someone who had participated enthusiastically in that sport. He had just graduated in law and was joining his father's firm.

The following morning was bright and sunny. George was taking a group of boys for a rugby class and playing in a match in the afternoon. Jackie suggested that she and Ruth go for a walk in Richmond Park and then go to cheer him on. Their route would take them past the Wright's house which was on a corner.

As they approached they could see Mr Wright trimming an escallonia hedge which fronted to the street. When they were still a fair bit off his face broke into a wide smile of recognition and he laid his shears on top of the hedge and came towards them.

'Jackie, why didn't you tell me that you were a friend of Ruth?' he scolded.

'Now, Mr Wright, you really cannot expect me to keep track of all your girl friends,' she teased. 'But I only found out that you knew one another at the beginning of this week so you cannot really accuse me of wasting time in bringing her to see you.'

'I won't and I'm so glad to see her. Now you must come in for coffee,' then he stopped. 'I'm sorry,' he went on, 'were you on your way to someplace?'

Jackie answered with a question. 'Has Mrs Wright been baking this morning?'

'As a matter of fact she has. She was just cleaning up afterwards and I was chased out of her road.'

'Then we weren't on our way to any place of importance.'

Mrs Wright, wrapped in the aroma of fresh baking, came to the door. If Ruth hadn't been told of her ancestry she might not have known that Mrs Wright was of mixed race. Her skin was almost white, but it was her dialect which surprised most. She had a soft Scottish burr and many of the expressions were similar to ones that Ruth had heard from her father.

'My mother was Nyanga, but my father was a Scot,' she explained in answer to Ruth's question.

'When he was first in Nyasaland he hated it because he could see nothing but land no matter where he looked. His folks had an estate in the middle of the Kintyre peninsula and when I was wee he used to tell me that in lambing time he could see ships coming in from the Atlantic in the morning and from the same spot in the middle of the afternoon he could see them going up the Firth of Clyde.

'Then he managed to get a big tract of bush land on the shore of Lake Nyasa and brought this into cultivation. My mother was the daughter of one of his men and she became his housekeeper. My father used to joke that I was one of the better products of progress. As bush was cleared game were driven off. An old lion turned man eater. It was dangerous for my mother to go home after sundown. There were only the two of them in the house. The rest followed naturally. They never married.' She stopped for a moment, then went on with a catch in her voice. 'Mum died when I was six. Dad had a sister, Aunt Betty, who lived in London. He sent me to her so that I could be educated here. I took a degree then went back to Nyasaland to teach.'

She turned to reach for the hand of her husband before going on.

'There I met this old goat who in those days was a young buck.'

CHAPTER 7

The visit was so enjoyable that Jackie and Ruth abandoned the idea of a walk in Richmond Park and didn't leave until it was time to go to watch the rugby match. They only got away after giving a promise to return very soon.

The two girls became firm friends and fell into a comfortable pattern in which Ruth spent around one weekend a month with the Murrays. This arrangement found particular favour with George and his rugby-playing friends and the older Murrays noticed with some amusement that the number of dirty coffee cups in their kitchen sink always increased on the weekends when Ruth was there.

As the end of the first academic year approached, Ruth considered going home for the summer, but abandoned the idea as being too expensive. Her friendship with the Murrays and the Wrights meant that she didn't suffer from homesickness and her parents, who wrote alternately, assured her that everything was well with them.

One letter from her father gave both pleasure and amusement. 'Iain and Anna drove out at the weekend to leave Sarah with us,' he wrote. 'Your mother enjoys having her and this will be her last chance of a long break before she starts school. Both Iain and Anna look well and the domestic arrangement seems to be a success. So much so that your brother has a broody look in his eyes and I'm almost certain that I can hear wedding bells above the jungle drums. Your mother gives me a row if I mention it but I'm sure that she will be as pleased as I, and I know that you will be if it comes off. We'll keep you posted.'

On a visit to Richmond just before the end of term, Mrs Wright brought up the subject of how the girls intended to spend the summer.

'I have a particular reason for asking. Our daughter, Helen, has just discovered that she is pregnant again. She is suffering badly from morning sickness and young Jimmy is at a stage when she can't take her eyes off him. The summer is a busy time on the estate with hay making and harvest and her husband, Tommy, has more than his hands full. It looks like there may soon be an election and Jim cannot get leave. I don't want to leave him on his own.

'What all this is leading to is simple. Would you two be willing to give up part of your holiday and go up there? I can assure you that it is a lovely area,' she ended somewhat hesitantly.

Thus it was that at the end of July the two friends found themselves aboard the sleeper train from London to Glasgow. They would then have a boat trip down the Firth of Clyde to Campbeltown and the last leg of their journey would be by car. Ruth had never travelled by train and the idea of going to bed in one was something of a novelty. At first she found the clack of the wheels on the rails to be irritating but, as the train built up a steady speed, the noise became more soporific and her eyes closed. She awoke to the sound of voices outside as Jackie poked her head over the edge of the top bunk. She realised that the train had stopped and said so.

'Of course it has, silly. It stopped an hour ago when you were still snoring your head off. We're in Glasgow.'

Just then there was a tap at the door and a steward came in bearing a tray loaded with tea things. He stumbled over the sill and gave an exclamation in Gaelic. As he put down the tray Ruth thanked him in the same language. He turned to answer, saw the colour of her features, and without speaking scuttled out the door.

'What on earth did you say to him?' asked Jackie. 'He looked as though he had seen a ghost.'

'Well, he spoke in Gaelic when he caught his foot and almost dropped the tray. Dad was taught Gaelic when he was little and when he and Uncle Roddy and Uncle Lachie were together they spoke Gaelic to each other. Iain and I just picked it up as children. I just wished him good morning and thanked him for bringing the tray. It was when he saw that I was black that he began to doubt his ears. He'll have something to tell his wife when he gets home. Will there be Gaelic speakers where we're going?'

'I don't know. My geography teacher was a Scot and he used to tell us that there were areas of Scotland where Gaelic was still the main domestic language but I don't know if Kintyre is one of them. Anyway, we'd better get a move on. Even in Scotland the boat won't wait.'

And so it was from the sea that Ruth saw an area which was to have much influence on her life. It was a dull, rather raw morning when they left Glasgow and as the vessel advanced to full speed off Gourock both girls were pleased that they had taken Mrs Wright's advice to wear trousers. But as they rounded Arran, where red deer gazed down from the hills, the sun broke through. A young officer of the crew joined them at the ship's rail and pointed out the landmarks. Ruth thought that the tree covered hills were similar to parts of Kenya. The young man told them that the other side of the peninsula was more fertile and much more intensively farmed.

They passed Davaar Island and entered the sheltered bowl of Campbeltown Loch with the sun slightly behind them and eased their way to the pier through a screen of wooden hulled fishing boats.

Carrying their cases the girls picked their way down the steep gangway and as they got to the bottom a squat, strongly built young man was waiting to meet them.

'Hullo, I'm Tommy Fraser and you must be Ruth and Jackie,' he said.

'And I'm Jimmy,' said a voice at knee level and a miniature edition emerged from behind his father.

As Tommy Fraser bent to pick up the cases, his son ranged himself between the two girls and held up a hand to each of them. And so they progressed, one, two, three and swing, to a new green Land Rover that was parked at the top of the pier. As Tommy loosened the ropes which fastened the canvas cover to the rear door, a collie dog with a broad white strip down its face leaned out to lick his hand.

'Will he be alright in there?' Ruth said anxiously as the father hoisted up his son.

'Oh, yes. This is how he travels. Look,' and he indicated a palliasse with a sackcloth covering which was placed on the floor behind the front seats.

Then, 'Lie down, Roy,' he ordered and the dog did so at one end of the mattress. The child, who was obviously used to the manoeuvre, stretched out with his head cradled behind the foreleg of the dog. The canvas was securely fastened and the three adults climbed into the front seats. As they cleared the town, Ruth looked into the back. The wee boy was sound asleep. The dog saw her glance and his tail rose and fell once as though in reassurance.

A bare four miles north west saw them looking out from the Atlantic coast. Although there was little wind there was a heavy ground swell from some deep water storm and the sun pierced the spume to make rainbow colours as the waves crashed on the rocks.

Tommy Fraser was a steady driver and an entertaining companion and they seemed to have been travelling for a mere ten minutes instead of more than half an hour when he swung off to the right and followed a gravel drive bordered by hawthorn hedges on both sides. At the end it opened out to reveal a massive lawn. Set back from this and crowned by pine trees which rose into the hill behind was a beautiful granite-built mansion house. Tommy stopped the jeep when he heard Ruth gasp and they sat for a moment as the sun wiped the last of the recent rain from the rough stone. Then Ruth felt herself begin to giggle before stopping in embarrassment.

'I'm sorry,' she said as Tommy turned towards her. 'Uncle Lachie used to tease Aunt Kate about having 'big hoose' manners. That is certainly a big house.'

'Many a time we wish that it was smaller,' he said. 'It costs a fortune in upkeep. One day soon the roof will have to be renewed and I try not to think about it.' Then, 'Ah, there's Helen,' as a young woman came out to stand at the top of a short flight of broad stone steps.

Helen Fraser had taken her height from her father and her broad open features from her mother. As yet she showed no signs of her pregnancy and she greeted the two girls with enthusiasm.

'If I follow the same pattern as last time I'll be fine after the third month,' she told them, 'but just now the only thing that I can keep down is porridge and normally I hate the stuff. With Jimmy it was custard and I haven't been able to stand the sight of it since.'

In the afternoon Tommy was going to cut grass for haymaking and Jimmy began to cry because Roy was to be locked up in the kennel. Despite the tantrum, his father wouldn't budge.

'When I was about eight or nine years old I had a dog just like Roy,' he explained to the two girls. 'One day the ploughman was cutting weeds with a horse mower. A couple of boys from the village had come up and we were playing football at the edge of the field. Spot set off after a rabbit, ran into the blades of the mower, and had both his forelegs sliced off just below his knees.'

He paused a moment, his eyes bright, before going on.

'At that time we still had a gamekeeper and he was sent for to put Spot out of his pain. This was a man who had served in India with the regular army and come back to fight right through the Great War.' Another pause before going on with a burst. 'I've seen it far too many times since then but that was the first time I found that grown men can cry and I can still hear the echo of that shot.'

Unnoticed by the rest, Jimmy's tears had stopped as he listened to the story. He slipped off his chair and ran round to climb on Tommy's knee.

'Daddy, I don't want Roy to die,' he said as he threw his arms round his father's neck.

CHAPTER 8

When Ruth and Jackie were loaded in to the Land Rover on the first leg of their return journey to London they found it hard to believe that their stay had lasted seven weeks. As they wound their slow way down the gravel drive before turning on to the main road, the minds of both girls cast back over a holiday which, although neither quite realised it at the time, had sown the seeds of a love of Scotland which ultimately would alter their lives.

At the time of their arrival green had been the dominant colour. Now the hay fields were again green and white dotted by grazing lambs. But some of the grain fields had already been cleared and neat stacks were appearing close to the farm steadings. Some had rows of stooks like soldiers on a parade ground and on the few fields where grain was still standing tractor drawn binders were at work.

The Frasers' estate, which had been passed on from father to son over more than two centuries, covered an area just short of eighteen hundred acres of hill and forest and almost two hundred acres of what was termed low ground.

'We have a dairy herd of Ayrshire milking cows and also a herd of suckler cows who rear their calves on the hill during the summer months,' Tommy had explained. 'That is why we have to make so much hay and grow oats and turnips for winter keep. The hill ewes forage for themselves summer and winter, but we bring the ewe lambs, which are going to be used for stock replacements, down to the low ground for their first winter.'

'Have you any horses?' asked Ruth. 'Uncle Roddy has more than a dozen which he uses for roundups in Kenya.'

Tommy smiled. 'No. We just have collie dogs and we can't sit on them. Horses wouldn't be able to move quickly enough on our hills. It's much too steep and rocky. We used to have eight horses for the farm work, but now we have only two and they are of an age where they aren't fit for much. But they were such good friends that I haven't the heart to get rid of them as long as they are enjoying life.'

For the first three weeks of their stay, Ruth and Jackie had tried to do most of the cooking between them. But by the end of that time Helen's bouts of sickness had almost stopped and whenever the weather was good she insisted that the girls got outside as much as possible. If the farm task of the day was something they could join in they did so, but at other times they went down to the beach where they taught young Jimmy to swim.

As Ruth had often gone with her father to help out on Roddy MacLean's farm in Kenya she wasn't squeamish when any veterinary work had to be done among either the sheep or cattle, but Jackie admitted to having more interest in the handsome young vet than in some of the gory tasks that he was performing. One of the shepherds did persuade her to attempt to clip a sheep but when the job was only halfway completed the animal got to its feet and ran off with the fleece trailing behind like a train.

Their easy laughter and willingness to tackle anything made the girls popular with the farm men. Ruth had been so accustomed to mixing with white people that she really wasn't conscious of the colour of her skin, but for the first few days she felt that the older men in particular were shy of her. One especially hot day, the hay which Tommy had cut on the day of their arrival was ready to be built into miniature stacks in the field. As the men worked, the girls crawled round the bottom of the ricks and pulled out any loose ends and when the pile was built into a conical shape which would shed the rain they helped to put on cross ropes. When the men went off to begin the process again, they raked down the finished rick. One of them, a tall man in his early sixties, but still with a full head of grey hair, was particularly handsome. He still carried himself very erect and Tommy had told the girls that he was an ex-guardsman and had resented being told that he was too old for military service in the '39 war.

Ruth was raking down the rick which he and his companion, who was of similar age, had just finished building. She was wearing white shorts and a white top. As the men walked away she heard the tall man say in Gaelic, 'Man isn't she the real beauty the black one.'

Almost as a reflex action she heard herself say in the same language, 'Och, and isn't it yourself that's not too bad either.' The other man had just applied a match to his newly filled pipe. It dropped to the ground and spilled out all its tobacco before the tall man recovered enough to burst into laughter.

Later, at the afternoon tea break, he returned to the subject and Ruth explained about her father's adoptive parents and Roddy and Lachie MacKinnon.

'Lachie MacKinnon, was that a doctor who was killed in an accident a few years ago? His wife was killed as well. Her own name was Kate MacEachern?' The statement was in the form of a question and his voice was excited. Then he finished in a quieter tone. 'He was a Sgiathanach and the wife was an Ileach.'

'Yes. Did you know them?' Ruth was surprised.

The big man hesitated, obviously conscious that everybody else was now listening, before he went on with another question. 'Do you have a brother who took a law degree in London?'

'Yes, I do.' The mystery was becoming deeper.

'Lass, I can hardly believe this. Neil MacEachern was my mate in the army. Ten days before the war ended he was killed. When I got home I went to see his wife. Kate was just ten years old and was their only child. Her father was only seventeen when she was born and her mother had just turned sixteen. She had a hard time.'

'I never thought about this before but is Aunt Kate's mother still alive?' asked Ruth.

'No, and she was the last of her line. She had been ill for about a year before Kate died but she never told her daughter.

She wrote me a letter when she got the news of Kate's death and I went out to Islay the following day.' The voice of this big, phlegmatic man broke before he went on. 'Mary died an hour after I arrived.'

He took a minute to compose himself before turning to look Ruth full in the face.

'She isn't here to tell you how much you and your brother meant to her. I'm just so pleased to be able to do it for her. She blamed herself for Kate having neither brother nor sister and was much worse when Kate had no family of her own. 'Now,' he said to the other man as he rose to his feet and pulled his pitchfork out of the ground, 'this isna puttin' boots on the bairns.'

'That was as much a surprise to me as it was to you,' Tommy Fraser told Ruth that evening. 'I knew that big John had a friend on Islay who had died but he's quite a secretive man and I never guessed that there was such a story behind it.'

'I wonder why they never married.'

'No, I don't find that surprising. Many women in this part of the world feel that to marry again is being disloyal to their dead husband.'

Shortly before the Christmas break she received a letter addressed in beautiful copperplate handwriting. It was from John MacKinnon and he enclosed a photograph .

'I know that I should have consulted your family before I did this,' he wrote, 'but at my time of life time is not the most plentiful commodity. I trust that you will forgive me in the knowledge that Mary MacEachern, Kate's mother, will I am certain be looking down with approval.'

The photograph was of a headstone of polished granite. It was obviously taken with care and the inscription was clearly visible.

'SACRED TO THE MEMORY OF MARY MACEACHERN WIFE OF NEIL KILLED IN ACTION NOVEMBER, 1918, MOTHER OF KATE AND GRAN OF IAIN AND RUTH'

Ruth knew that her father had worried about his children being sole beneficiaries of the estate of Lachie and Kate. He had been reassured by big Roddy that this had the full approval of Lachie's family, but the thought persisted in his mind that there might be relatives of Kate to whom some of the money might have been useful. She had the letter and photograph copied and sent off the originals to Samuel. She also wrote a long letter of reply to John MacKinnon.

But the next letter came from Helen Fraser.

'I have bad news for you. Big John MacKinnon is dead. He had a boat with which he did some fishing when things were slack on the farm. Last Thursday morning he set off in good weather. There was a fresh wind in the afternoon but nothing compared with some of the gales he had coped with. He lived alone, but had an elderly neighbour to whom he always gave a shout in the evening and for whom he left coal and kindlings for the morning.

'When he never appeared, she raised the alarm. The Islay ferry found his boat just to the west of Gigha on Friday forenoon. The wind was south easterly and his body was found on Texa just before dark on Friday afternoon.

'This is a small island just outside Port Ellen on Islay. Tommy went out on the afternoon ferry yesterday which was Saturday.

'He has just phoned me,' she continued. 'The funeral is on Wednesday on Islay. He is to be buried beside Mary MacEachern. There are no close relations on either side and Tommy feels that this is what they both would have wished.

'John brought your letter up for us to read. Please believe me that you brought great joy to the last days of a man who was a born gentleman.'

Ruth looked at her watch. It was half past two on the Wednesday afternoon. She wept for a man who she had hardly known and for a grandmother of whose very existence she had been unaware.

CHAPTER 9

Just before the Easter break, Ruth had a letter from Iain. He and Anna planned to get married in July and he wanted his sister to come home for the wedding. For Ruth the London spring passed slowly and crawled into summer. It was almost two years since she had left Kenya and she longed to see her parents.

At last the day came and Jackie saw her off at the airport. Rome, Cairo, Khartoum and finally Nairobi. Ruth climbed down the steps from the plane to see a tall, handsome African couple standing in the shade of the airport buildings. The man's rugged features were topped by a head of iron grey hair. The woman was almost as tall as the man but her burnished face and black hair showed none of the worry signs exhibited by the man.

Between them and restrained by a hand on either side there danced a beautiful child of early school age. As the wee girl was released and started to run towards her, Ruth realised that it had taken her a second or two to recognise her own parents and then Sarah. Anna's daughter had doubled in height in the two years that Ruth had been in Britain. Ruth was shocked by how much her father had aged in that same period.

'There have been rumblings of trouble almost since the time that you went to London,' Naomi explained when she and Ruth were alone. 'So far they have been able to contain it but for the past eighteen months we had a man in charge of the security forces who didn't help matters. It was a stupid appointment. He had never been to any of the African countries in his life. Not even for a visit. He never quite got round to a bull hide whip but I'm sure that he thought about it.'

'Is he still here or has he been recalled?'

Her mother laughed. 'I suppose that an accurate description would be 'voluntary repatriation'. He certainly seemed to have influential friends and any complaints about his conduct were being ignored. One day he went out to Roddy's farm while your father was there. Your father's dog was lying in the shade of the stoep. Instead of asking it to move this man kicked it and tried to push it aside with his foot. The dog had never bitten anyone before but it took a snip out of the official buttock.' She giggled again before going on. 'He couldn't sit down for a time so he had to be off work. The dog was six years old. Roddy and a group of farmers and business men prepared a citation recommending Alexander MacLeod, aged forty-two, for consideration of the honours list for services to the cause of peace in Kenya. It was done as a joke on a night when they had drunk too much, but they made such a good job of it that the authorities took it seriously.

'We got an official letter addressed to Alexander MacLeod. Your father opened it and it said that an award was being considered. He and Roddy went to Nairobi and got it stopped, but the story got out and the man became a laughing stock. He just wasn't big enough to deal with this and asked to be recalled.'

'Does Dad still have to be away from home so much?'

'Not now. Some of the younger men are taking over. Do you remember Jomo's son, Simon?'

'I'm not likely to forget him but the last time that I saw him he was working for a firm of architects and I quite liked him.'

Naomi nodded before she said, 'He has grown into an able young man and now he has quite a bit of influence. He and Iain have become friendly and he is going to be Iain's best man. A group of young men who have managed to get a foot on the career ladder are doing their best to keep the more volatile element under control. Simon is one of them. Your father feels that because Jomo is so respected his son will be able to build on this and will relate well to the younger men who are the real agitators.'

'Do they think that there may be real trouble?'

'Your father does. He says that in any situation there are always some who will try to exploit it for their own ends. There have been raids on some of the more remote farms already and he thinks many of these are done by villains who are only interested in stealing. But some of the raids have been particularly vicious. It's frightening and if they get away with it somebody else thinks that they can do the same.'

The wedding day was a particularly happy one for Ruth. Many of her school friends were there and all of the staff who could be spared from the hospital. Sarah was a flower girl but all of the time when she could escape from her official duties was spent with Samuel who she addressed as Seannair.

Simon Itombi was a real surprise. He had the height and weight which his boyhood had indicated but his manner had changed completely. From being extrovert and brash he had become quiet and mannerly. Almost shy. Both he and Iain were in formal dress and Ruth had to suppress a giggle when she remembered them as bare-bummed wee boys. When he greeted Ruth he bowed over her hand in a courtly gesture.

A broad shouldered young man with stubbly red hair and features which suggested time spent at the bottom of a rugby scrum wrapped her in a bear hug. He stepped back with his hands still on her shoulders and as she took time to recover her breath she recognised Alastair MacIntyre, one of the boys who had come to her rescue in the Cecil Barclay-Brian episode. He escorted her to a shaded table and went off to fetch cool drinks.

'Now,' he said when they were settled, 'tell a displaced teuchter all about life in the capital of the Empire. And where did you get to last summer? We thought that we had lost you.'

Ruth told him about her arrival in London and the episode which resulted in her meeting with James Wright and about her friendship with Jackie Murray. 'Dad often says that things work out for the best in the end and if it hadn't been for that horrible wee man I would never have met the Wrights.'

She went on to tell about her meeting with John MacKinnon and his connection with Kate and her mother. Just then Simon came past their table and spoke for a moment before going off to mingle with other guests.

'Now, there's an example of your father's maxim,' said Alastair as he looked after him. 'If that boy's father hadn't upended him when he did Simon would never have grown into the man he is now.'

'How do you know about that?' demanded Ruth. 'That was long before you knew him.'

'He told me himself. Cecil Barclay-Brian found his way into the conversation one night when a few of us were together. Simon felt that this was someone else who might benefit from parental discipline but that stupid mother of his would never allow his father to lift a finger to him.'

'Do you know where he is now?'

'Oh, yes. He's back here on the farm. The expensive school took some of the pomp out of him but his mother's influence has undone most of the good that they did. I feel sorry for his father. He's a really decent wee man. Anyway,' he went on, 'we can't be wasting good time talking about somebody who isn't worth the breath. You said that you had been to Kintyre. Whereabouts, and what did you think of it?'

Ruth explained at some length about the Wrights and the hard work being done by Tommy Fraser to get his estate back to being a viable business.

'What makes you so curious about Kintyre?'

'My grandfather came from there. He fought in the Boer War and instead of going home he wandered his way up through Africa and settled finally in Kenya. His own story was that he hadn't enough brains to be a farmer so they sent him to university. But I think that he was just among the last of the gentlemen adventurers. Anyway, he did very well once he settled here.'

He took a drink from his tall glass before going on. 'A few

weeks ago my father had a letter from a firm of lawyers in Campbeltown. It seems that the last leaf is about to drop off the family tree. This is an elderly lady. We are the only surviving relatives and she wants the Old Man to go across so that she can see him before she dies.

'There is an estate of several farms and a Home Farm with a mansion house. Iain has had dealings with this legal firm because of a client who died while on holiday there. He says that if they didn't write Magna Carta they could well have been consulted.'

Before leaving for London, Ruth spent a couple of nights with Roddy and Fiona at their farm. Both of their sons had left Kenya. One had married a Canadian girl and was now practising as a doctor in Canada while the other was farming in Australia.

'We would hate to have to leave Kenya before we are ready to retire,' they told Ruth. 'This country has been very good to us and we would like to put something back. But we are glad that the boys have moved off. At present there are better places in the world to bring up young children.'

'Once we know that they've got their numbers we'll do a world tour and visit them,' said Roddy.

His wife threw a cushion at him. 'He's always saying that,' she told Ruth angrily. 'You'd think that he was talking about a stock of cattle.'

Sarah cried and clung to Ruth at the airport. Ruth in turn embraced her father. Both Roddy and Fiona had assured her that they would try to keep him from doing too much.

'As we get older we need him more here and if we go off on holiday he'll have to take over so that should at least keep him at home,' said Roddy.

Nairobi had been warm and sunny. London was dour and cold but all her friends were bright and welcoming.

CHAPTER 10

The next two years passed quickly for Ruth. Although she was an able student she worked hard and never left anything to chance. Both she and Jackie were popular with the other students and there were few parties to which they didn't receive an invitation.

The summer after Ruth's trip to Kenya, they decided to explore some of the Scotland about which they had both heard so much. At the beginning of July they took an overnight train from London to Inverness. They found the old town both fascinating and friendly after the selfish bustle of central London and spent the morning wandering from shop to shop before buying pies and cans of soft drinks and making their way up to the castle.

The day was beautiful with a heat haze shimmering over the water below. After eating, they lay back on the sloping grass using their rucksacks as pillows. They had slept only fitfully in the train and soon tiredness overcame them. They awoke simultaneously with a sense of cold. The sun had moved round and they were now in the shade of the old castle walls.

'Let's just stay here and treat ourselves to a bed for tonight,' said Jackie.

Even as they crossed the bridge over the Ness the following morning they still hadn't decided which road to follow. They wanted to get to Kyle of Lochalsh for the ferry to Skye but had neither time limit nor route in mind. They had promised to end their holiday with Tommy and Helen Fraser but their return to London was almost two months in the future.

Shortly, they saw a road sign pointing to the right. 'That decides it. Beauty. That's what we came to see,' said Ruth.

Jackie laughed. 'It's BEAULY you idiot. Somebody has drawn a bar across the letter L.'

'Och, well, no matter. It looks like a quieter road. I vote we go that way.'

The day was hot and airless and when they were well on the open road they began to hitch for a lift. Several cars passed before a Land Rover driven by a ruddy-faced, tousled haired young man in his early thirties drew to a stop beside them.

'Where are you headed, girls?' he enquired in a cultured voice which belied his appearance. Then as they hesitated, 'I'm going to Dingwall. Hop in and you can think about it as we go along.'

The man introduced himself as Bob Hamilton. When the girls in turn gave their names it was obviously a surprise to him to hear a five foot ten beauty with a skin of burnished ebony say that she had the surname of MacLeod.

'Is this your first visit to Scotland?' he asked to cover what was becoming an embarrassing pause.

Jackie explained how and where they had spent their summer two years previously. He turned and looked at them both before a blast from the horn of an approaching lorry warned him that he was straying to the wrong side of the road.

'Tommy Fraser. Is that a man built like a Clydesdale horse that never quite reached its full height? And tell me, is his wife Helen?'

'The answer to the first question is a qualified yes. To the second definitely yes. They have two children. Tommy calls his family "a doo's clockin" which translates as a pigeon's pair. Obviously you know them.'

The latent question was ignored, then, 'There's a wee baker's and cafe in Beauly where the coffee is only bettered by the hot scones. Would you like to try it?'

There was a rustle as the vehicle stopped which told the girls that a collie dog had been lying behind their seats. Bob held up his hand palm outwards and the animal quickly lay down again as he closed his door. When he stepped on to the pavement they saw that he walked with the rock of somebody who had one leg shorter than its fellow.

'Now,' he said when they were seated at a table, 'tell me about the Frasers. How did you come to know them?'

Ruth explained about her meeting with Helen's father on her arrival in London and how the friendship had developed from there.

'Tommy and I first met up on commando training. Then we were sent in different directions and didn't get together again until well on in the war.'

He went on to tell how the pair of them had been sent to destroy a German fuel dump on the French coast. They had set timed charges but hadn't made it back to their dinghy when the first of them went off. This had alerted a command post and the Jerries opened fire.

'They could see us quite clearly and I got a bullet in my leg. I wanted Tommy to leave me but he wouldn't. He really is as strong as a horse and he just slung me over his shoulder. By the time he dumped me in the dinghy the fires were so bright that the crew of the M.T.B. could see the Jerry post and their gunner knocked it out. It wasn't until we were back on board that Tommy admitted that he had been hit. If there hadn't been an officer in the crew with medical knowledge he would almost certainly have died.'

They had been taken to the same hospital. Then Tommy's wound had developed an infection and he was moved.

'He came back to us after about a month,' Bob went on. 'He was down to almost eight stone. I've seen more flesh on a butcher's apron but he just didn't care. All he could speak about was this girl Helen. Then she came to visit him and we could all see why.'

Bob didn't appear to be in any hurry and when they were back in the Land Rover he turned to the girls before putting a hand to the ignition.

'There's a beautiful glen just a few miles ahead. You wouldn't have much chance of a lift because there's hardly any traffic. We can take a run up there if you like.'

'But what about your market?' Jackie protested.

'Och, there's plenty of markets but there's only one day like this,' was all the reply she got.

They veered left just after Muir of Ord and at Marybank a sign pointing west said 'Strathconon'. Bob drove slowly. He and Jackie kept up a desultory conversation. Ruth, who had time to absorb the panorama opening before her, thought that she had never seen an area of such beauty.

At first the land was flat and fertile with fields of ripening grain beyond the broad stretch of the river. Then a twisty part of the road took them into an area of scrubby woodland. Just then the dog rose to its feet and poked its nose over Bob's shoulder.

'Hold on a minute, Speed,' he said before drawing into a small lay-by.

They all got out and after the dog had snuffled around he came back to Ruth and lifted his head to be petted. As Jackie and Bob were talking, she started to stroll along the road and Speed went ahead of her. He left his card on various spots of interest then suddenly stopped, looking into the side of the road and with his left foreleg bent up to his body. Ruth moved quietly towards him and looked in the direction of his point. A small speckled deer calf looked back at her with more curiosity than fear in its large brown eyes. Jackie and Bob had seen her stop and she motioned them forward. They moved up quietly and still the calf never got to its feet but turned its head to the side in a quizzical gesture. After a moment, Bob put a hand on the shoulder of each of the girls and turned them away, then quietly snapped his fingers for Speed to follow.

'That was a roe deer calf,' he told them when they were back in their vehicle. 'The red deer is bigger and they seldom come this far down the glen. The mother won't be far away but if we had touched her calf she might abandon it.'

Shortly the glen opened out with forests rising to the tops of the hills on either side and mountains rising in the distance. Ruth commented on the different shades of green in the trees and Bob explained that this was a deliberate mix of spruce and pine.

'It looks lovely just now but looking back down the glen on a sunny autumn day is quite spectacular,' he told them. 'The pine softens to a golden colour and contrasts with the deep green of the spruce.'

About a mile farther on he stopped in the middle of the road, fished under his seat and handed a pair of powerful binoculars to Jackie.

'Look up the hill at about eleven o'clock and about three hundred yards out,' he commanded.

'What am I supposed to be looking for?' she asked after a moment or two as she brought the glasses down.

'See that grey rock,' he pointed. 'Look to the left of it and slightly higher. There's a red deer hind suckling her calf.'

'Why isn't she with a herd?' asked Ruth when it was her turn with the binoculars. 'In Africa a mother rejoins the herd whenever her calf can walk.'

Bob explained that in Scotland the adult red deer had no natural predators except man.

'I've known a hungry fox take a calf and also eagles when the calf is very young. But at that stage numbers aren't going to increase its safety. After a few days she'll link up with her group.'

They stopped on a bridge over the river to watch salmon swimming in a pool, then Bob pointed to a small stone-built hotel built on a rise off the road. 'Lunch,' he said without leaving room for discussion.

As they were walking up the short drive a man who was weeding a flower bed glanced at them then sprang to his feet with a broad smile.

'Captain Hamilton,' he said, 'what brings you to the more civilised parts of the kingdom?'

'I was going to say that it was hunger that made me stop here but seeing you makes me doubt my judgement,' laughed Bob as they shook hands. 'Girls, meet Sergeant Jock MacRae. He took me on a survival course when I was training for the commandos. Tommy Fraser was there as well. The things that he made us eat makes me hope that they don't let him near the kitchen here.'

The hotel owner appeared on the steps above them and offered to bring drinks out to the garden.

As the other three made their way to the bench, Bob limped down to the Land Rover, let Speed out and took him up to lie in the shade with them. Jock watched him until he had sat down then asked if his leg gave him much trouble.

'If ever I run out of money, and in farming that might not be a joke, I could take a job as a weather forecaster. The damned thing aches like blazes when it's going to rain. I often heard other people say this about their various complaints but it really does happen.

'Do you ever hear anything of Tubby?' was the next question.

'You can probably guess that Tubby is Tommy Fraser,' Bob said to the girls before going on to explain how they had been able to give him information which he imparted to Jock.

'Yes I knew that he and Helen planned to get married. She was lovely, but with parents like hers she couldn't be otherwise.'

'How did you come to know them?' Bob was curious.

'They used to visit us in hospital,' said Jock and lifted his left hand from his pocket. Only then did they see that the heel of the hand and the third and fourth fingers had been sliced off.

'I was brought in two days after you were discharged.'

He went on to explain that Helen's parents often visited Tommy at times when their daughter couldn't get off. They also spoke to all the other patients, but Jock, being a Scot, was a particular favourite of Mrs Wright.

The two men reminisced as they ate. Jackie slid down to the grass and began to share her food with Speed. Ruth gazed at the hills and thought how much they reminded her of her native Kenya. This glen was so peaceful and few cars passed to vie with the noise of the river as it voiced a gurgling protest

69

at being channelled through the bridge which carried the road over it. Far from feeling homesick, she began to realise that she could happily live in Scotland. This was her second visit. At times she was conscious of being stared at but this could be due to her height drawing extra attention to the colour of her skin and here were two men whose only reaction had been to her name being unusual for someone who was obviously African.

Eventually they all moved down to the Land Rover. As the two men stood still talking the girls were examining the hill to the south through alternate turns of the binoculars. 'I wonder if we could camp here for the night,' said Ruth. I'd love to walk on these hills. They look as though nobody has ever walked on them before.

When they re-voiced their idea, Jock turned to Bob. 'Can you leave them a bit farther up the glen?' he asked.

'Of course.'

Jock went on to explain that he only worked a couple of days a week in the hotel gardens. The rest of the time he spent stalking and doing gamekeeper work with one of the estates. On the following day he intended walking out to the hill to the north of the glen to check on stags which would have to be taken out in the cull which was soon due to start. He would pick them up in the morning and walk out with them to within sight of Achnasheen.

'Make your camp at the boathouse,' he told them. 'There's plenty of twigs for a fire at the edge of the loch and the deer and the sheep have the ground so bare that your fire won't get away.'

It took them almost two hours to cover the dozen miles to the top of the glen and it was a reluctant Bob who finally turned back down with only Speed for company. The girls had told him that they intended to visit Skye and Islay before going on to Kintyre. He held Jackie's hand in both of his as they said goodbye.

CHAPTER 11

The girls had set up their tent, climbed the hill until the tent was but a dot below them, made a fire, cooked, ate and washed in the sun-warmed waters of the edge of the loch before settling down to enjoy the spectacle of the setting sun. The light darting off the gentle ripple of the water reminded Ruth of similar spectacles in Kenya but it was a novel situation to Jackie.

'There's not a whisper of sound except natural ones,' she said in a low voice. 'If I was suddenly transported to the centre of London now the shock would kill me.'

It was still light when they wriggled into their sleeping bags and were soon asleep. After what seemed a very short time Ruth awoke to snorting sounds close to the other side of the canvas. A glance at her watch surprised her by telling her that it was just after four in the morning. Gently she parted the flap and looked into the eyes of an antlered stag. The beast made off up the hill in company with a group of its fellows. Jackie slept on undisturbed. Ruth snuggled down and did likewise.

Jock arrived just before eight o'clock but the girls had already breakfasted and packed up ready to go. He looked with approval at the doused fire which had been built on the gravel of the shore of the loch. He then went to the back of his jeep and returned with an empty rucksack which he placed beside the girls' backpacks.

'Split half of the weight of one of your packs into that,' he ordered. 'You can take one each and I'll take the other.'

The girls protested but he wouldn't budge. When this had been done he hoisted the full pack on to his back and spent some time adjusting the straps. When he was comfortable he returned to his vehicle and produced a haversack which he slung over his left shoulder and patted into position. Next, to balance the right shoulder, came a rifle which showed the shine of much care. As the girls each shouldered their lightened burdens he looked up. 'Now,' he said, 'the Psalm is number 121.'

As he led off Ruth started to sing 'I to the hills will lift mine eyes,' and he stopped.

'Where did you learn that?' he asked.

'Och,' she said in Gaelic, 'That's a story that I'll tell to you some time,' and he laughed in surprise.

They hadn't climbed for long before the girls were grateful to Jock for lightening their burden but he set a steady pace and didn't seem to notice the weight that he was carrying. From time to time he stopped and swept the hill above with a brass telescope which he produced from the haversack. This he passed to the girls if there was anything of interest to see. At one point they watched a pair of golden eagles resting with motionless wings on a thermal just above the skyline and a small, fluttering bird which Jock told them would be a newly flighted chick.

Several times they saw hinds with young calves. After studying one group of deer for a moment, Jock was just bringing down his glass when something caught his eye. After a moment he passed the telescope to Ruth. 'About a couple of hundred yards to the right there's a flat rock,' he said in a low voice. 'Just above it there's a hind suckling her calf.' Ruth watched and could see the froth from the rich milk drip from the lips of the calf. Just after she passed the telescope to Jackie an eagle passed over the hind in a fast swoop, dropped to the heather and rose with a grouse firmly held in its talons. Startled, the hind turned. There was a clearly audible crack as she fell over. When she struggled upright her near hind leg stuck uselessly outwards.

In what was a continuous flow of unhurried movement, Jock shed the haversack, unhitched his rifle and dropped on one knee. A shell came from his belt and was rammed home. The report was loud in the girls' unexpectant ears. The heavy bullet threw the calf off its feet and slammed it into the hillside. Came the sharp click-clack of the bolt as he ejected and reloaded, another sharp report which didn't seem as loud as the first, and the mother crumpled beside her offspring.

'Damn,' said Jock explosively as he rose to his feet with the rucksack still on his back. The whole incident hadn't spanned more than ten seconds. He looked at the girls. Jackie had large tears running unheeded down her cheeks, but Ruth appeared calm.

'Why did you shoot the calf first?' she asked with a slight quickening of her breath.

'If it had run off it might have been too far away for a clean shot before I had another sight of it. I'm just glad that we were here. The two of them could have had a slow death.'

He glanced at Jackie who wiped her cheeks with the back of her hand. 'I'm sorry, Jock, it just happened so quickly. But,' she added, 'we were on wards just before the holidays. A lot of the people we saw there would be grateful for the quick end you have just given to these two animals.'

They climbed on for another half hour then Jock stopped and turned. 'Do you want a last look at Strathconon for this trip?' he asked. From this height Jock's jeep looked like a small knot at the end of the long ribbon of the road. After a stretch of fairly level ground scarred by peat bogs he stopped again and pointed. The ground sloped away and they could see the sun glint off windows in the distance. A train was puffing its way through the glen leaving a trail of smoke and they heard it whistle at a level crossing.

Jock shed his loads and produced flasks and a packet of sandwiches from the haversack. 'Are you married, Jock?' asked Jackie as he unwrapped two mugs and placed them beside his spread. 'I was,' he said quickly. Jackie coloured when she realised that she had stepped on ground which shouldn't have been disturbed.

As they sat on the sun-warmed slab of rock, the talk was companionable. Ruth told of her early life in Kenya and how she had learned Gaelic as a child and had come by the name of MacLeod. She spoke of Roddy MacLean and Lachie and how they and her father used to converse in the ancient language. The soft summer air seemed to draw words out of her and she told more of her life than Jackie had ever heard.

It then seemed natural that Jock should follow on. His ancestors had been from Strathnaver but had lost their land in the Highland Clearances. Like many others they had made their way to Glasgow and become part of what was almost a community in exile. Jock's father had become a schoolmaster and he himself was born in Kenmore. As a youth he and a friend had spent their summers cycling. They had camped by Loch Tay and Loch Rannoch, watched sunsets from the tops of Ben Lawers and Schiehallion, had their tent blown from above them in Glen Lyon and had developed their knowledge and love of the hills and wild life.

He had just graduated from Glasgow University when the war started and had immediately joined up. He had met Bob Hamilton and Tommy Fraser while doing a spell as instructor at the commando training ground in the Great Glen. While there he had met a girl who was a nurse at the hospital in Fort William and they had got married. They had been married just under two years when he had been wounded. His wife had come down to see him in hospital in Weymouth.

He glanced at Jackie before going on. 'She had to travel through London on her way home. It was the time of the flying bombs. She was killed. Rather than put it in a letter she had come down to tell me that she was two months pregnant.' Jackie caught her breath in a sob and it sounded loud in the sudden silence. After the war he couldn't face the thought of going inside to work.

'Watch where you pitch your tent tonight,' he said as they redistributed their packs. 'There will be rain before morning.'

Both girls hugged him before they set off downhill with an exhortation to be careful. By the time they got down to level ground their legs were aching. They went to a croft house to buy milk which they weren't allowed to pay for. And as a bonus were given two hot scones straight off the girdle. They were told to make their camp on a bank above where a gurgling burn splattered from rock to rock before resuming its more sedate course some twelve feet below. They both awoke in the grey light of the summer night to the rattle of rain on canvas. The gurgle of the burn had accelerated to a gentle roar. Drugged by weariness they went back to sleep.

The overnight rain had cleared the air and the sun poured from a clear sky by the time the girls had packed up and taken to the road. The packs had become heavy and sweat was dripping as a small ancient lorry clattered to a stop beside them. The driver was bare footed and his only apparel was a pair of shorts which had seen much service. He explained that he was Australian, had travelled across America over a period of a year taking work as he could get it and had then sailed to Southampton where he bought his vehicle. He was funding his tour of Scotland by working as a sheep shearer. 'My great-grandpop was sent to Australia as a convict. He was from a place called Bethnal Green. Oh boy, but he made a good move. He had stolen a chicken because his mother was ill and the family had no money. I went to see the house where they had lived.' He steered his way round a ewe and her lamb before going on. 'They sent him from there to Perth as a punishment. If the old codger had stolen a turkey he might have been sent to heaven.'

He had an easy conversational style and as he divulged his life story he extracted a similar fare from his passengers. He also had been a medical student but had quit at the end of his fourth year. At first he had been reluctant to give a reason but a full blooded young man has little chance against two similar girls and the story came out. There had been a bush fire close to his parents' farm when he was on a weekend break. The hut of an aborigine family had been caught in the flames. No doctor was available and he had gone to help.

'There was a mother and father and their kid, a little girl of two years. I don't suppose you've ever seen Abo kids, but at that age they're beautiful. Lovely little smiling faces and

75

big eyes.' His voice was toneless as he went on. 'The parents had lain down together with their baby beneath them. They were both dead but the baby was still alive. Her skin crackled as I picked her up and she screamed.

'I carried her nearly half a mile to a truck that was to take her to the landing strip. She screamed all the way. Every bloody step. Almost a thousand of them and every one jarred through that little girl's body. When I laid her on the floor of the truck she gave one more scream and died.'

The ancient vehicle trundled on with nobody speaking for a time before he resumed.

'Why are we so cruel to one another? If that had been a poddy I'd have shot it as soon as I found it. But I had to turn that kid's last hour on earth into pure hell just because she belonged to the dominant species.'

'Will you go back to study?' It was Ruth who asked the question and the reply was instant.

'Yep, I wrote to my old Prof. from the U.S. and his reply was waiting for me at Aussie House in London.'

He shot a slightly defiant glance at the two girls then, 'I'm going to specialise in burns injuries.'

It was a reluctant chauffeur who dropped his passengers at the end of Strathcarron where he turned in towards his next job. As they were saying goodbye a train drew in to the station. 'Do you know where that train is going?' asked Jackie.

'Yes, Kyle of Lochalsh.'

'Right.' Both girls picked up their packs and ran.

That evening they camped at Sligachan in the shadow of the Cuillins of Skye.

CHAPTER 12

Ruth had heard much about Ramasaig from Roddy and Lachie but felt unprepared when she saw it in reality. As she stood in the ruins of the township from where their ancestor had been driven almost a century before, she could imagine the angry, despairing shouts of the men and the screams of the women and children. The quiet murmur of the burn as it shuffled to the sea only served to enhance the sense of obscenity.

They pitched their tent in the lee of a large rock close to the shore and after supper sat outside to watch the sun ooze its way towards America between the tops of Hecla and Beinn Mhor on South Uist. A ship passing northwards through the Minch set up a series of ripples and the colours danced towards them like rainbow hued lambs. It was late but still light when they reluctantly closed the flap of their tent. When Ruth awoke she felt refreshed but her watch told her that it was barely four o'clock. Without wakening Jackie she slipped outside and had a quick wash and a drink of cold water from the burn before she dressed.

An almost full moon was following the path of the previous night's sun as she wandered along the green flat of the machair past the mounds of stones which were the only memorial on the graves of people whose descendants would now be enhancing the population of every corner of the world. She stood for a time looking out to sea before turning uphill towards the roofless stone walls which were all that was left to tell the story of a once happy community. These walls, now welded together with moss had been built with such skill that they had long outlasted the people who had first caused them to become empty shells. Men like Roddy MacLean and Lachie MacKinnon who had grown from the seed of this place were a richer tribute and memorial to their ancestry than that enjoyed by many who had so mercilessly evicted their forebears.

Ruth wandered in and out of the small buildings which she thought to have been family homes. At times she paused and she tried to imagine the people who had once lived, loved and laughed there. Then she came to a larger building apart from the others. A large coping stone had fallen off the west wall and lay inside. She sat down on this. The first rays of the early morning keeked over the east wall to warm the top of her head. The building would have been a school or a church or perhaps a combination of the two plus a meeting place for entertainment.

She imagined grave adults and disciplined children sitting in solemn rows. She imagined happy and boisterous children playing games. Just at the other side of the roofless gable the burn chortled over a mini-waterfall. As she became conscious of this sound she remembered some of the children's rhymes which Lachie had taught her so long ago and found herself fitting them to the music of the water. She thought of how much Lachie would have enjoyed being here with her and she wept. And she wept for the cruelty which was raging among her own people and hoped that like Roddy and Lachie their descendants could resurrect triumph from tragedy.

Jackie had a crackling fire and a smell of fresh brewed coffee to greet her return. Over breakfast they decided that since the weather was so good they would explore the north of the island. At the end of four very pleasant days, which included a night on Raasay, they found themselves on the ferry from Armadale to Mallaig.

As they walked to the head of the pier they saw a cafe with tables outside on a balcony. The smell of cooked fish and chips won them over. Without a word they climbed the four steps and took their seats at a table. They had almost finished their meal when Ruth felt a pair of hands lightly cover her eyes before being taken away. 'G'day sports,' said an exaggerated voice and the smiling face of Grant Metcalfe, their Australian friend of the week before, appeared between them. He was going to spend a week working on Mull before going back up north . There he had a fortnight's work lined up, then it was back to London for a few days' sightseeing before the long trek home and back to study. 'Where are you pair headed now?' he asked.

'Islay next,' replied Ruth, 'but how we get from hence to yon has yet to be decided.'

'You look very tidy compared to us,' observed Jackie taking in his crisp cream coloured shirt and khaki shorts.

'Yep,' he grinned, 'the lady in my last digs took pity on me and laundered all my clobber. I've booked into an hotel for tonight. If I have a bath night and morning I'll be almost as clean as my clothes by tomorrow. Are you two going to camp? And do you know where?' as they nodded.

'Somewhere close,' it was Jackie who answered. 'I want to watch the fish being landed. Dad used to take me to Billingsgate when I was small.'

'Right. I'll get the truck. We can tootle around and find a place without you having to carry your packs.'

They found a spot which had a view of the harbour. Ruth went to the wee croft house to ask permission. She came back with a broad grin on her face and a paper bag containing half a dozen hot pancakes in her hand.

'When the old lady was coming to the door she spoke in Gaelic. I answered her, but when she saw my face she wasn't willing to believe her eyes. She scuttled back to get her glasses. I have to call in the morning to get fresh milk and eggs for breakfast.'

Grant then told them that he had the next two days clear and planned to use them to explore Ardnamurchan and Morvern before taking the ferry from Lochaline to Mull.

'The father of one of our neighbours comes from a place called Ockle. He had always intended to take a holiday to go back but died last year. I promised his son that I would take some photographs for the grandchildren. If you would like to join in I can pick you up in the morning. The ferry from Lochaline goes back to Oban and you should manage to pick up lifts south from there.'

The chauffeur-driven limousine picked them up just after nine in the morning. Albeit at a more purposeful speed, Grant had travelled the route a few weeks before so the scenery wasn't new to him but the mid-summer colours on a sunny day were like a fairyland to the two girls. The sands of Morar looked tempting to swim from but they decided not to make a stop so early in the day. Progress was slow as they looked at broods of duckling being shepherded by fussy mothers and seals basking on the rocks. Twice they had to stop to allow clutches of pheasant chicks to get off the road and bury them-selves in the heather.

Grant produced binoculars to allow them a better look at a circling golden eagle and as they turned south at the head of Loch Ailort a family of four young otters entertained them to a cabaret from the pebble shore. A few miles further on they saw a strip of white sand trapped between big rocks and extending out to the water and it looked an ideal picnic spot. As they carried things down, a small red sports car with the hood down stopped on the roadside just in front of their vehicle. Ruth looked back to see two fair haired young men studying them intently. When Grant turned round the car drove off but they heard coarse laughter above the roar of the exhaust.

It was past the middle of the afternoon when they drove through a herd of grazing red deer to turn into the road to the township of Ockle. They had passed groups of ruined houses which mutely told the sad tale of people long gone and Grant was relieved to find that his photographs of Ockle featured homes still occupied and people going about their business. He was also able to talk to two old men who remem-bered the man who had gone to Australia almost half a century before.

They decided to visit Ardnamurchan lighthouse before looking for a place to camp. Grant, despite the protests of the girls, announced that he was going to cook supper and stopped at the shop in Kilchoan for milk and supplies. As they passed a small hotel they saw the red sports car and the two young men drinking at an outside table. They spent over an hour at the lighthouse taking photographs and admiring the view. As they came back to turn left towards Sanna Bay they again saw the car parked about a hundred yards back from the crossroads but gave it no thought. When they reached the bay, Grant parked his truck between two sand dunes.

'Now,' he said as he turned to the girls, 'this looks like a good spot to bivvy.' When they both nodded, he went on, 'I'm going walk-about. If you girls want a swim, supper could be more than hour away. I had a good wash this morning,' he finished with a grin.

They pitched their tent before changing and going for their swim. The incoming tide was warmed by the sand and by the time they came out they could see twin spirals of smoke rising close to their tent. Ruth noticed that one column was wider than the other. When she got near she discovered the reason. A skillet bubbled on one fire, but the other was covered by a thin flat stone which was supported at either end by two other stones which held it a few inches above the burning wood. On this hot plate was laid three silver fish. As the fat dripped from them it sizzled on the hot stone.

'Mackerel,' explained Grant in answer to her question. 'I caught them off the rocks just round the corner. They're the easiest fish to catch. If you held out a frying pan they'd jump into it.' He looked up at the two girls with the sea water still glistening in beads on their bodies. 'Can I take a photograph of you two standing by the truck?' he asked hesitantly.

'Better wait till we're dressed,' said Ruth.

'Oh, no,' as he rose to get his camera. 'I want to boast to the Sheilas back home. Without a photograph they won't believe that I travelled with a couple of stunners like you two.'

'Bring your tinnies when you're dressed,' he told them after taking several photos.

When they returned, the fire had been allowed to burn down until only grey ash was left. Their chef took their tin plates, slipped a fish on to each then, with a twig raked three large roast potatoes from the ashes beneath and added one beside each fish. From the skillet on the other fire came sliced carrots, then from beside the back wheel on the shady side of the truck appeared a bottle of white wine. 'Just watch the spuds. They'll be hot,' they were warned.

When the first course was disposed of Grant gathered the plates, poured some hot water into each from the skillet and then scrubbed them with heather before drying them with a cloth. Each plate was handed back to its owner adorned with a mound of fresh strawberries. Before he sat to take his own sweet one of the fires was freshened and the skillet, with powdered coffee and water, was set to boil. Jackie thought that she had never had a meal quite like it and said so as they lay back to watch the sunset.

They became absorbed in the spectacle and paid no attention to the sound of a car drawing on to the grass not far from where the girls lay spaced with Grant between them. The short grass and the muted crackle of the tide on the sand had muffled any footsteps and the first hint of trouble to the girls came when they each found one of the young men from the red sports car standing at their feet. The faces of the two carried the glow of alcohol.

'Say, Bud,' said the one nearest to Ruth in a Deep South voice, 'don't you know it's illegal to transport black monkeys outside a cage?'

Grant had been lying back with his hands clasped behind his head. Drugged by the view and the contentment of the previous moments he took a second or two to sense danger. The American reached forward, caught Ruth's cotton shirt and pulled. As she sat up the garment slid up to her shoulders exposing her bare breasts. As Grant rocked forward to gain his feet the other man kicked him viciously behind the ankles and sent him sprawling again.

But years of handling bush reared cattle which had been brought into corrals had sharpened his reactions. As he fell backwards he continued the momentum and rolled heels over head to become upright. It happened so fast that the two men were still ogling Ruth as he started forward. The man who had kicked him was first in line and he was felled with a short uppercut which cracked like a pistol shot when it landed.

But the fellow who had attempted to humiliate Ruth was not getting off so easily. He was treated to a slow succession of open-handed slaps to each side of his head which drove him relentlessly towards the water. As his eyes began to glaze, Grant spun him round, seized him by the shirt collar and the seat of his beautifully creased trousers and ran him into the sea. Again he was pulled round and a final slap with a clenched fist to his temple tumbled him sideways. His head went under but when he sat up the water only came to his waist. Grant watched until the man struggled spluttering to his knees then turned and walked back to the others. He arrived to find Jackie sitting on the other man's legs while Ruth knelt on his back with his right arm bent up between his shoulder blades. An opened flick knife lay on the grass a few feet away. Grant picked it up, went back to the edge of the sea and flung it as far as he could into deeper water.

'Let him up,' he commanded the girls when he returned. 'Look,' he continued as they hesitated, 'you can't sit on him all night. Just let him up and I'll talk to him.'

The fellow struggled to his feet, glared for a second or two, then rushed. Grant stepped aside and clipped him as he passed. Then, when he turned he was given a similar dose of medicine as had been received by his friend. When he finally backed into the water a hefty push to his chest dumped him on his beam end. His tormentor watched for a moment to satisfy himself that any further threat from the pair was unlikely then calmly returned to the girls. They noticed with surprise that his breathing had barely quickened despite his exertions.

'Now,' he said, 'if you two could wait there for just a moment or two I'll see our guests on their way.' As they watched he started the sports car, swung it round and reversed down to the edge of the sand. After walking into the water to the two men, who were still on their knees, the girls heard him speak but couldn't hear his words. Whatever was said, he yanked the man who had had the second bath to his feet, marched him to the passenger side of the car and opened the door. The lower part of the man's body was hidden by the door but the two girls saw Grant bend down and heard a short scream before the American collapsed on the car seat.

The second man was brought up, a similar tableau enacted, only this time the scream was louder, before he was deposited in the driving seat. As the car was driven slowly past, neither of the men looked towards the girls but they could see that the faces of both were contorted in agony.

'What did you do to them?' asked Ruth.

'I take it that you two know what they intended.'

'Well, yes,' said Jackie. 'They certainly weren't just going to tell us the story of their lives.'

'Australians are among the most free living folk on earth but characters like that just aren't tolerated. A couple of years ago a swagman interfered with two young Abo girls from a village close to our farm. The two mothers caught him in the act and dealt with him. The brother of one of them is my cobber and he told me what they did. What I did won't be quite so permanent but that pair won't have much interest in the girls for a week or two.'

'Do you think they may come back later tonight?' asked Jackie anxiously.

'No, I don't. But I'll draw the truck round and sleep beneath just in case.'

'Oh, no you won't. What if it rains?' protested Ruth. 'We've each got sleeping bags and if you're going to be our guard dog you are sleeping inside our tent in comfort. Don't worry. We won't attack you.'

The tall lean Australian burst into laughter. 'Why did you have to spoil it by adding that last bit?' he said.

Each girl kissed him goodnight as he settled in the space between them. They spoke for a short time before decorously falling asleep.

CHAPTER 13

Early in the evening the girls stood on the after deck of the car ferry and waved a reluctant goodbye to Grant as he stood on the pier at Craignure. They had wandered back along the shores of Loch Sunart and through velvet antlered stags on the narrow road of the Morvern peninsula before having to sprint for the last ferry from Lochaline. They had seen no sign of their assailants of the night before.

On landing at Oban the lure of a hot bath saw them easing their way through the crowds of holiday-makers towards the youth hostel on the esplanade. On that short walk, Ruth thought that she had heard snippets of every language in the world. They dined on fish and chips while sitting on the rocks by the shoreline before taking their cameras to view the sunset from McCaig's Tower. At the top of a steep flight of steps which had taken them up the cliff face they stopped to take a picture of the vast roofless colosseum-like stone structure.

An old man, who was sitting on a seat, heard them speculate as to its origin and in the way of the helpful local world-wide began to tell them the story. It had been built around the turn of the century by a wealthy philanthropist and had given work to many men who were badly in need of it. The heavy blocks had been shipped in to the harbour and their journey up the steep hill to the place of assembly had been by iron shod carts pulled by Clydesdale horses. As Ruth looked at the gradient which had to be overcome she imagined she could hear the ring of the hooves and smell the sweat of these powerful animals and the encouraging shouts of the men who cared for them.

When they reached the tower the lower rim of the sun was being kissed by the mountain tops of Mull. They watched the myriad of colours change second by second as the fiery ball sliced itself off on the peaks of ancient volcanoes. Just as Jackie captured the last tip of light in her camera, someone jogged her elbow and she turned to receive an apology from a tall, deeply tanned and fiery red-haired young man. As he spoke, Ruth stepped alongside Jackie and his face burst open in astonishment.

'Ruth, where in hell did you spring from?'

'I'm not sure where it might be in hell, but we've been touring Scotland for the past ten days.' Then she turned to her friend. 'Jackie, this is Alastair MacIntyre from Kenya. He saved me from a fate worse than death when I was fourteen years old. Now,' she added, 'can you tell us how you come to be here?'

Alastair explained that he was on a meandering route to visit an aunt. When he explained where, the surprised girls realised that it was only a few miles from the Frasers in Kintyre.

'But I'm not alone,' he said gesturing towards one of the ports in the wall of the building. The girls looked to see a young black man sitting with his legs dangling outside. The corner of the sketch pad on which he was engaged could be seen over his shoulder. Alastair whistled sharply through his teeth. A few final strokes of the pencil, the legs were swung inward and Ruth looked into the smiling face of Simon Itombi who she had last seen at Iain's wedding.

Explanations emerged over coffee. The two had met on the plane from Kenya the week before. Simon had won the flight to Britain and a couple of hundred pounds of spending money in a design competition. Alastair had a hire car waiting for him and had offered a lift in return for company. They had toured up the east coast and right round the north of Scotland and landed in Oban the previous night. Their day had been spent on a sail to Iona aboard the 'King George'.

Simon was starting his journey south by train the following morning and Alastair was going on to the official part of his visit. When he heard of the girls' immediate plans he offered to leave them at West Loch Tarbert in time for their ferry to Islay on the following day.

It was late in the afternoon when they sailed up the water filled rift of the Sound of Islay which separated the island from the spectacular peaks of Jura. The fast north running tide bore their ship along with the éclat of a speedboat. The hamlet of Port Askaig with its sleek little hotel suddenly came into sight like a child discovered during a game of hide-and-seek. A bus took them to the centre of the island. They camped by the shores of Loch Indaal and were lulled to sleep by the gentle lap of the water and wakened in the morning by the calls of the wading birds marshalling their young. Ruth had been born and spent her young life in an area where the only sounds were natural ones but to Jackie the small tidy cemetery to the south of Port Ellen seemed to be the most peaceful place in the entire world.

The twelve mile journey from their camp site had consumed an entire day. They had stocked up their supplies in Bowmore before the Round Church above the village drew them like a magnet. As they shed their packs to take photographs from the gate, two old pipe-smoking men who were sitting on a seat discussed them in Gaelic quite unaware that Ruth could understand most of what they said.

'Man, but isn't it the black one that has the grand back for a peat creel,' said the first as he gazed at the sky as though commenting on the weather.

'Och, yes indeed,' said his companion, 'but the other hasn't always been able to reach the trough. Her wee legs would never be able to hold a full pail of milk off the ground.'

The pair were still enjoying the sunshine when the girls came back after walking round the churchyard. As Ruth was swinging her knapsack to her back, one of them, again with his eyes on the far distance, said something which, because of the rustle of her effort, she didn't hear. But the innocent expressions on the two corrugated faces told her that she had been the subject of comment.

She shrugged her burden into comfort then turned round. 'Tell me,' she said in Gaelic, 'what is the difference between a peat creel and a herring creel?'

The old man's mouth dropped open and both he and his companion looked so contrite that the girls again dropped their packs and squatted on the grass to speak to them. The men were native to Islay and were fascinated by Ruth's story. Both had known John MacKinnon who was of similar vintage to themselves.

'But, och,' said one 'isn't it just the pity that you didn't meet Iain Mor earlier. Then he could have taught you God's Gaelic instead of that stuff from Lewis.'

'Och, yes,' came from his companion. 'Lewis Gaelic. Like tripe without onions, chust.'

When a rickety red bus appeared with a card stuck inside the windscreen giving its destination as Port Ellen, the girls were almost as reluctant to leave as the men were to see them go. But as they drove along the flat straight road past where piles of peat were drying before being carted off to add their distinctive reek to the local whisky, the driver proved to be equally entertaining. He had married an Islay girl during the war.

'They say that no matter who a Port Ellen girl marries she will eventually bring him back to where she was born.'

He was obviously a happy immigrant and like many people who adapt to a new location he had gone to a lot of trouble to acquaint himself with the local history. There were quite a number of small hollows in the old cemetery which were the only memorials to the people who were buried beneath. There were also many slabs of grey stone from which any inscription had been long since erased by the weather, but the granite headstone which marked the grave of Kate's mother was easily readable. At the bottom the name of John MacKinnon had been added. As they read the inscription Ruth and Jackie found that they were talking to each other in whispers as though their voices were an intrusion on the peace of the dead.

When they boarded the ferry at Port Ellen the following morning the captain was standing at the top of the gangway greeting his passengers. He was a solid wee man with a leg at each bottom corner and a face which bespoke a lifetime of good humour which had been helped by a fair amount of good whisky. The girls rid themselves of their burdens and came back to speak to him. When Ruth asked about Texa island and where John MacKinnon's body had been found he told them to come to the bridge once the vessel was under way and in open water.

The island was just coming up on the port side when they got to the bridge. While still keeping an eye on his helmsman the skipper took them out to the wing with a pair of binoculars and pointed out the exact spot. His friendly appearance turned out to be a mirror of his character. Like most of his crew, he had started off his working life as a deep-sea sailor. Gentle probing soon brought out the fact that Ruth was Kenyan and he told them that on his first trip, which had taken him away from home for a year, one of his ports of call had been Mombasa. Ruth's surname excited his curiosity and by the time he had extracted her story the ship was rounding the south end of Gigha and the girls had to leave the bridge in order for him to concentrate on bringing his vessel alongside a tricky pier at low tide.

Once cast off, they were allowed to rejoin him and when he discovered that they were going to the Frasers he summoned an engineer who was going on leave and organised a lift for them.

'This poor man comes from Campbeltown, but, och, he can't help that,' he told the girls, 'but we're training him in more civilised ways, aren't we, Hector?'

'Aye, captain, for better or for worse,' said the young man as he went back to his duties.

Young Jimmy Fraser observed them with all the solemnity of his five years as they walked up the drive then, with a squeal, ran towards them. His mother appeared at the top of the steps with his sister by the hand but as they climbed towards them the wee girl hid her face in her mother's skirt. Her shyness was short lived and by the time that they had deposited their packs she was waiting at the bottom of the stairs.

When they joined Helen in the kitchen she told them that they had a fellow guest. Bob Hamilton had been in touch after meeting the girls and had arrived the night before.

'You girls seem to have made a hit,' she told them. For the next few days he did much for the enjoyment of their holiday. He organised a day trip to Gigha and they walked down through what the Norsemen had called God's Island and marvelled at the sub-tropical plants in the grounds of the laird's mansion.

Again by boat, they sailed from Campbeltown to Davaar Island which shelters the loch and makes it such a safe anchorage. Once there, Bob found some difficulty on the bouldered shore but when they gained their objective the spectacle which met them made the effort worthwhile. Many years before a painter had painted the scene of the crucifixion on the rock wall of the cave. As they stood in awe a ripple of sea was caught by the sun and for a few seconds reflected on the painting like a spotlight. Several people in the group crossed themselves and two women knelt to pray on the jagged rocks of the floor of the cave.

On the day before Bob had to leave they organised a picnic hamper and took the canvas cover off the back of the Land Rover. Helen and the two children took the front seats beside the driver. The two girls sat on a bale of hay in the back with Roy at their feet and a course was set for the Mull of Kintyre lighthouse. Jimmy protested that he wanted to travel in the back but Bob smoothed things over by telling him that he needed him to show the way.

Shortly after they turned off the Southend road they had to stop at a farm to allow a procession of domestic ducks to cross their path. As they passed through an estate and past a mansion house the road led sharply upwards. Bob stopped at the top to allow them to enjoy the view back over Sanda Island and Ailsa Craig to the Ayrshire coast which could just been seen through the haze.

The view when next the sea was visible made them catch their breath. The road seemed to project over a cliff and gave the impression of a sheer drop to the lighthouse several hundred feet below. Despite the beautiful day they could clearly hear the crash of the Atlantic swell in the rocks which were hundreds of feet lower than the lighthouse. Rathlin Island lay like a surfaced whale straight ahead and to their left the spires of Ballycastle could be seen over the hump of the Irish coast. Jimmy squealed with excitement as they inched their way downwards.

'How did they get all the materials here?' Ruth asked the lighthouse keeper who showed them round.

'Horse and cart from Campbeltown,' he told them. 'It's a round trip of forty miles. When they got down to better roads on the way back the men slept in the carts and the horses knew the road so well that they just plodded on home.'

They picnicked on the sandy beach in the lee of Dunaverty. The children slept on the road home. Ruth and Jackie bathed one each while Helen was cooking. Their father had been dipping sheep and waited his turn for the bath.

After their evening meal Bob and Jackie drifted outside. Much later Ruth went to the front door and in the fading light she could see the two sitting close together on the balustrade.

CHAPTER 14

The sheer splendour of graduation day took Ruth by surprise. The various dignitaries decked in their finest regalia made her think of tribal chiefs on festive days and increased her longing for her parents to be there. Even the more boisterous of the students, wearing their robes and carrying their soon to be added hoods, seemed subdued by the solemnity of the occasion. When it came her own turn to step forward the Tu Quo Que of the principal seemed like the ceremonial bestowal of a knighthood.

The night before had been spent at the Murrays. Jackie's parents had invited the Wrights to share in the celebratory dinner. James Wright was his usual mannerly self but during the meal Mary, his wife, appeared to be anxious. There was a sheen of moisture on her olive features and she continually glanced at her watch. Jackie and her mother were clearing away sweet plates and Ruth had just risen to help when the telephone rang. Hugh Murray and James Wright suddenly struck up a conversation and the former turned to Ruth.

'Can you answer that?' he said. 'If it's someone for me I'm not in.'

There was a silence and she was just about to replace the receiver when a deep and familiar voice asked, 'Is that you Ruth?'

'Dad,' she shouted, 'where are you?'

Again a pause then, 'We are in Iain and Anna's house in Nairobi. Your friend Mr Wright organised this so that we could congratulate you. Have you decided on your next move?'

'Yes, I'm going to do surgery at Hillingdon.'

'Well, don't be in too big a hurry to work out here, This isn't the country that you left and I fear for the future. Now

I'll hand you over to your mother. Take care. We're proud of you.'

When she had spoken to the rest of the family Ruth returned to the table and kissed James Wright soundly on the lips.

'It was Mary's idea, but I enjoyed that much more than she would,' he laughed.

Ruth's only regret was that Jackie was going to take up a post in Inverness. The friendship between her and Bob Hamilton had developed to romance and she wanted to be nearer to him.

One of the senior surgeons was from Bridge of Orchy and he teased Ruth about touring Scotland and not going through Glencoe. He was nearing retiring age and as a result of standing for long periods had arthritis in both hips. This caused him considerable pain and at times some of the staff found his gruff manner a bit intimidating though Ruth loved him.

'Never forget that you are working at an operating table and not a butcher's slab,' he exhorted his students. 'The patient is a person, somebody's mother, father, son or daughter and some day could be you. Treat them with respect.'

Although he wouldn't again be able to walk the hills of his youth he intended to spend his retirement in his birthplace. 'I won't need to walk. The capercaillie will fight outside my kitchen window in the spring and the stags will roar outside my back door in the autumn,' he told Ruth.

Surgery was followed by an intensive course in zoonoses and tropical diseases. After another long year of hard work she was given six weeks leave which would allow her to get home to spend Christmas with her parents and Iain and Anna's son who was now eighteen months old.

Her father looked much better than on her previous visit. Roddy and Fiona MacLean had gone on a tour of their family. First they had gone to Australia then were travelling home to Skye via their doctor son's home in Canada. It would be nearly two years before they expected to be back in Kenya.

'There is a young Scottish couple staying in their house,' Naomi told her daughter. 'Their name is Sinclair and your father has appointed himself as their guardian. He spends more time there than he does at home.'

'He looks well. Is he less involved in other things?'

'Much less. Simon Itombi, son of Jomo, has organised a group of younger men and so far they have been able to contain any trouble. Your father is still called on to settle many disputes but he is now seldom away overnight.'

During the next few days Ruth learned more about the tenants at the MacLean's house. Her father told her that the young man was a civil engineer in charge of the building of the extension at the airport. He was from Kintyre and his mother was a school teacher there. His wife was from Edinburgh, was a qualified vet and was in the last stages of pregnancy.

'She is now very heavy and the heat is making life difficult for her,' Samuel told his daughter. 'It is not good that she is there alone all day. Boredom is making her look for jobs to do when she should be resting.'

A week later Ruth found herself accompanying her father as he went to the MacLean's house in the morning.

'Elaine's blood pressure is causing worry and her doctor wants to take her into hospital,' said Samuel. 'Her mother is coming out but won't be here for another two weeks. If you can come until she gets here and is rested then Elaine would be able to stay at home.'

A tall handsome young man met them at the door and invited Ruth inside. His wife was fair-haired, fair skinned and beautiful but when Ruth saw her she was reminded of a word often used by the old Scottish surgeon. That was 'trauchled'.

Over a cup of tea the two girls learned something of each other. Elaine told how she and her husband, Davie, had met. She had a sister, Kay, who had been sent to Canada for safety at the start of the war. The ship had been torpedoed by a German submarine off the coast of Ireland.

'The ship was loaded with women and children,' she told

Ruth. 'Two days later a shepherd saw Kay's body floating in the sea off the Mull of Kintyre. His dog swam out and drew her in to where he could reach her with his crook. This man, Ian Boyd, worked with Davie's father. At that time we lived in Ipswich. I was two years younger than Kay and would have been on the same ship, but was ill and not fit to travel.'

She went on to tell how she and her mother had gone to visit the Sinclairs after her parents had moved to Edinburgh. She laughed. 'At that time Davie was a big, gawky, country boy and, of course, I was a city girl and the last word in sophistication.

'Both his parents were lovely and Ian Boyd, who found Kay, was a real gentleman. There was more brain power in that house in the hills than would be in the home of any academic in the country. And, of course, there was Jock. There are fifty million people in Britain but only one Jock Spence. By this time my father was drinking heavily. It did my mother so much good to find that Kay's body had been cared for by such a family.'

As she talked and recounted the family history, Elaine visibly relaxed. Seeing this, Ruth made no move to interrupt her flow of talk. Thus she heard how Davie's father had died of polio just as his only son was due to go to university and how his mother, Marie, lived on a croft with a view across the North Channel to the Irish coast and of her life as a teacher in a small country school.

The story switched to Edinburgh and Elaine's own family. Her father had been a metallurgist who had done important work during the war but then couldn't face the competition from younger, able men and had turned to drink. He had been able to break the habit for a time then had lapsed again. Then, suddenly, he had committed suicide by swallowing barbiturate tablets which he had taken from Elaine's veterinary bag.

After his death they had learned that he had advanced liver cancer and couldn't have lived for more than a few weeks. Her mother, Katherine, had gone back to work as a lawyer.

Throughout the narrative there were occasional mentions of Ian Boyd who had found Kay's body and of his wife, Jean, and their family. Lighter parts were punctuated by the name 'Jock Spence'. So much so that Ruth's curiosity overcame her natural reticence and she asked the question.

Elaine smiled, 'Really, Davie and I will never be fatherless bairns as long as Jock is alive. Nor will our mothers be widows. He grew up in a Glasgow tenement but his mother died and he settled in Campbeltown. Some day I hope you may meet him.'

During the next two weeks this became a routine pattern for Ruth and Elaine and after the morning chat Elaine was sent to bed with a book and her carer busied herself with cooking and housework. 'We must have you fit to enjoy your mother's visit,' Elaine was told.

'I have never seen a mother and daughter who resembled one another so much,' Ruth told Katherine Stark when she arrived. 'If I had met you at the airport I would have known who you were.'

'Is Elaine as well as she looks?' Katherine asked next morning when Ruth brought her breakfast. 'Oh, yes, She's a naturally healthy young woman. Part of the reason for the rise in blood pressure was that she was inventing work because of the boredom of being alone all day.'

'Are you going to be here for the birth?'

'No, sadly, not unless she's early. I'm off back to London two days before the baby is due.'

Ruth returned to the kitchen and it wasn't long before she heard the voices of mother and daughter in conversation. She smiled to herself. Elaine wouldn't need her to talk to this morning and she could get on with other things. Suddenly there came a scream from the bedroom followed by a muffled crumbly crash. She ran through to find Katherine staring in horror at her daughter who was lying partly on her side on the floor.

'She was standing on the bed to tack up the end of the Christmas decoration when she snagged her foot on the sheet,' the mother answered her question. 'The back of the chair caught her full on the stomach as she fell,' she added with a slight rise in her voice.

Ruth became aware of a spreading pool of moisture on the polished wood of the floor.

'She's going into labour. We'll lift her on to the bed.'

Ruth parted Elaine's dressing gown and lifted her night-dress. An angry red bar stretched across her stomach from hip bone to hip bone. Then she was aware that Elaine had opened her eyes.

'If I had known that you wanted so much to have me here for your delivery I would have given you a bottle of gin,' said Ruth. 'Now I'll get Dad to send a message to Davie and the doctor while he fetches my bag.'

Samuel returned with her emergency kit bag and the news that the doctor was attending a confinement at a remote village and that Davie had gone off to chase up a contractor.

'The men have deserted us,' she told the other two. 'Anyway, we shouldn't need them for this part.'

A quick examination showed that nothing was going to happen for some time and the foetal heartbeat was strong and regular. Ruth left Katherine sitting with her daughter and went off to make some preparation for the evening meal. Several times she checked the heartbeat then, almost four hours after she had fallen, Elaine announced that the birth was imminent.

'Now,' she told Ruth firmly, 'I've delivered many animals and this won't be much different. It's just that this time I'm going to be at the other end. Just keep me up to date with progress.'

When the head emerged Ruth felt uneasy but continued murmuring encouragement to her patient. A slight pause in progress when the hip bones of the baby came against the pelvic bones of the mother, an urgent order to push, and Ruth had a baby in her hands. Without pausing for expla-nation she hastily wrapped the small body in a towel and ran to the kitchen.

Laying her burden on the table she had her worst fears confirmed. The baby was dead and the parchment texture of the skin told her that it had been dead for some hours and that any attempt at resuscitation would be useless. Yet a bare ten minutes ago she had been listening to a strong steady heartbeat. Grabbing a clean towel she ran back through to the bedroom.

Elaine started to speak but Ruth interrupted.

'How do you feel?' she asked.

'I feel as though I'm going to do the whole thing all over again.'

Ruth glanced down but this time what she saw was two tiny feet. 'Push, Elaine, I'll explain later,' she said as she grasped the ankles in her right hand and placed the left on her patient's stomach. It would be difficult to say which of the three women lost the most sweat during the next few minutes.

Katherine held her daughter's hand, counted to five, exhorted her to effort, then repeated the process. Ruth was caught by the need for urgency in a breech delivery and the danger to the hip joints of the baby which was pulling back its feet in a reflex action as though it resented being disturbed. Then she had the shoulders.

'Once more, Elaine,' she shouted and then sat back on her heels taking the towel with her. Mother and daughter heard a gull-like cry then the tall black doctor rose to her feet and laid a towel-wrapped bundle in the crook of Elaine's arm. 'Mrs Sinclair, allow me to present your son.'

Ruth waited a few days until Elaine was on her feet and confident in handling her baby. Then she spent a week with her parents and three days with Iain and Anna before returning to London. Jackie met her at the airport. 'You'll have to take more leave in the summer,' she said. 'Bob and I are getting married in June.'

'Well, don't get pregnant for a while. I have decided that I don't like doing deliveries for friends.'

CHAPTER 15

Bob Hamilton and Jackie Murray became man and wife on a beautiful June day. The wedding was conducted by a Scots minister who had been padre to Bob's regiment. Jock MacRae was best man and Ruth was bridesmaid. The Frasers were there with their two children. There was a bus-load of farmers, shepherds and gamekeepers along with wives or girl-friends who were either neighbours of, or workers on, Bob's estate. The whole Scottish contingent looked so ruddy and healthy compared with the Londoners that Ruth remarked on this to a skin diseases consultant who was at the hospital on a six months' secondment from Edinburgh.

'Have you been to Scotland? Surely you have with a name like MacLeod?'

Ruth told him of her two visits and how much she had enjoyed them and loved the country.

'Well,' he said, 'there's a post coming up at our tropical diseases unit at the beginning of next year. If you want to apply for it I'd be happy to recommend you.'

On a sunny day in late September she stood on the ramparts of Edinburgh Castle after having had her interview. In the distance she could see the orange of cleared harvest fields contrasting with the street bustle in the foreground. An anxious five weeks later she received confirmation of her appointment with effect from the beginning of February. Straight away she wrote to her parents telling them that she would be with them for Christmas.

So, for the second year in succession Ruth was able to escape part of the British winter for the warmth of Kenya. Her father said that he hadn't told the Sinclairs that she was coming so that she could surprise them.

As she walked the well worn bush path towards their house

her mind went back to her horror of a year ago when she realised that she had just delivered a dead baby girl. Then came the joy of a healthy boy. And she remembered the fortitude with which Davie and Elaine had accepted their son as compensation for the loss of their daughter.

Young Donald Sinclair was taking his first wobbly steps. His other granny, Davie's mother, was visiting and at first he was hesitant about coming to Ruth. His mother's obvious pleasure in seeing the person whom she claimed had saved his life on the day he was born soon overcame any shyness. When Ruth got talking to Granny Marie she realised with surprise that she could picture her house by the roadside in Kintyre.

'A few years ago Bob Hamilton drove us to the Mull of Kintyre lighthouse for a picnic,' she told Marie. 'It was a lovely day and we had stripped the canvas cover off the Land Rover. There was a wee man mending a fence close to that house. I particularly remember because we had the Fraser's dog, Roy, with us and that man had a beautiful collie dog sitting beside him. We all waved and he waved back.,'

'No doubt Davie and Elaine have told you about Jock,' Marie's statement was also a question.

'Yes, indeed. Elaine described him as adoptive father to both of them.'

'Well, the wee man that you saw would be Jock Spence. Both Katherine and I would have found widowhood to be much more difficult without him. And neither Davie nor Elaine would ever do anything which might incur his wrath.'

It was snowing when Ruth arrived in Edinburgh. The following day the sun shone and the castle looked like something from a Grimm's fairy tale. Her new post was quite exacting but she managed to spend at least one evening a week with Katherine. The latter encouraged the visits as she was feeling the big house to be lonely on her own.

'I'm going to spend a few days with Marie over Easter,' she told Ruth one evening. 'Would you like to come with me? We spoke on the phone last night and she told me to ask you.'

They travelled by train to Glasgow and bus to Campbeltown. As Ruth stepped off the bus a wee, wide-smiling, dark haired man came forward to meet her with outstretched hand. 'Hello, you must be Ruth.'

Ruth took his hand then delighted Katherine by curling her left arm round his shoulders and giving him a quick hug. 'And you must be Jock,' she told him. 'Elaine and Marie have told me so much about you that I feel that I know you already.'

'Ach, ye shoudna be payin' heed tae whit they weemin tell ye,' he said as he turned to greet Katherine before taking their cases and leading them towards a shining black Ford Consul.

He was obviously pleased when Ruth commented on the comfort of his car. 'Ah've ta'en this week on holiday when ah kent ye were comin',' he told them. 'Ah plantit Marie's tatties yesterday an' tidied roon her doors the day. Ah've got the next fower days clear an' the weather is lookin' tae be good. Ah'll be able tae let ye see a bit o' the country.'

Marie prevailed on him to stay the night. At first he said that he would go home and come back in the morning but Ruth tipped the balance.

'I want to see the sunrise from Cnocan Lin,' she told him. 'I need you to show me the way.'

He smiled. 'Lassie,' he said, 'Ah see ye ken hoo many teeth my Granny had. Ah'll bring ye a cup o' tea aboot six in the morn's mornin'.' He looked at the other two, 'Ony mair volunteers?'

They both laughed. 'No, Jock,' said Marie, 'We'll have your breakfast ready when you get back.'

Through the mists of comfortable sleep Ruth heard a gentle knock on her door. A pause, then her nostrils picked up the smell of hot toast and Jock was standing at her bedside with a tray.

'Ah'll gie the dogs a wee turn. Juist come oot when ye're ready.'

'Can we take them with us?' she asked when she appeared at the door and Jock ordered the dogs back into the barn.

'Better no'. There'll be newly lambed yowes up there an'

the dogs might disturb them.'

It was still half light when they passed through a gate on the roadside and started to climb beside a glen. After about five minutes Jock pointed to a flat slab of stone which was placed upright close to the burn.

'Did Elaine tell ye aboot Benny, ma ferrit?' he asked with a smile.

'Yes, she did. Why don't you have one now?'

'Ach, well, there's nae need. I first got a ferrit at the time o' the depression. My auld man wisna weel an' I wisna auld enough tae earn money. So I got a ferrit tae catch rabbits. Then he died an' the war cam on. The wee nyaff that did ma medical said that I wasnae fit for the forces so I came here. Wan o' the hotels wis a naval hospital an' I worked there as a kind o' Johnny-a'-Thing. I had taken Benny wi' me. We used tae go an' catch the odd pair o' rabbits for the kitchen.'

He smiled before he went on. 'A lot o' the young lads there had terrible wounds. It often wisna' easy to get them tae eat. It got tae a stage when Angus Graham, the surgeon, used tae send me oot tae get a pair o' rabbits to see if that wid tempt them.'

They were steadily climbing yet Ruth noticed that the wee man's breathing rate never altered despite keeping up a constant flow of speech. 'At first auld Erchie the gamekeeper wis juist a dampt nuisance. Ah wis forever having tae dodge him. Then wan day I hadna got anythin' by the time that ah had tae go back for ma shift. That day ah really needed tae get somethin'. We had a young lad, juist eighteen, an' were feart we were goin' tae lose him.

'As I was goin' doon the hill ah met Erchie. He asked if ah hadna caught anythin' an' ah wis so seek o' mysel' that ah telt him the story. I could see his bicycle doon at the roadside but when ah left him he turned back up the hill.

'Ah wisna lang startit tae work when ah got a message tae go tae the kitchen. The cook wis juist startit tae skin a broon hare an' there wis a pair o' rabbits hinging fae a hook. Fae then on we were good pals an' had many a crack. He had been a regular army man in his younger days.'

By this time they had gained enough height to see the Moil hills ahead to their left. They were passing quite a number of ewes, most of which seemed to have twin lambs. At one point Jock made a detour to avoid a mother busily licking a pair which were newly born. Ruth could hear her murmuring gently with a purring sound as she worked. When they reached the top Ruth understood why she had heard so much about this spot when she was still around five thousand miles away from it. She felt a swift pang of sympathy for Davie and Elaine in the heat and dust of Kenya. The sun hadn't cleared the horizon and Sanda Island lay dark and lifeless like a dead whale in the water, but far to the right it was teasing the Irish coast and softening the land to a duck egg blue. Then it rolled higher and they were bathed in its light. The hills behind them became burnt orange softening to lime green in the more fertile valley. To their left a grouse rose and far below a cock crowed, the sound rising in the clear, still air.

Jock was standing slightly higher than Ruth. She moved close, put her arm round his shoulders and laid her cheek against his. 'It's beautiful, Jock, really beautiful. Thank you,' she said.

They started down by a different route. As they jumped a ditch a ewe which had been lying behind a whin struggled to its feet then flopped back on to its side. The grossly swollen head of a half born lamb protruded behind it.

'Poor brute. We can't leave her like that,' said Ruth anxiously. 'Can you catch her, Jock?'

As he moved forward she again rose unsteadily but a quick run was enough to secure her.

'Just keep her lying comfortably on her side, Jock.' Then, after a careful examination, 'Do you have a sharp knife?'

'It's sharp but maybe no' that clean. Whit ur ye goin' tae dae?'

'It won't need to be sterile. The head has been presented but the legs are still inside. Because the head is so swollen I'll have to amputate it in order to deliver the rest of the lamb.

The quicker we work the less suffering there will be for the mother. The lamb is dead anyway so there won't be much blood. It won't bother you, will it?'

'Lassie, ah spent five years in a hospital. Juist you get on an' don't worry aboot me. Here, ye can kneel on this,' and he slipped off his waterproof jacket.

Ruth tucked up her sleeves then warily tested the edge of the knife on the ball of the thumb. Then going to a nearby hazelnut tree she cut off a small twig. After making a short split in the end she held the ends closed with her fingers while she drew the blade several times through the split.

'Not quite up to a Lister standard of hygiene, but that'll have to do.'

A few firm strokes and the knife was closed. In less than half a minute the carcass of the lamb was lying beside the head.

'Just hold her for a minute or two, Jock, there may be another lamb.' Then, 'Yes, we're in luck and this one looks to be alive.'

After a few moments a live, spluttering lamb was laid at the nose of the ewe and Jock eased her on to her chest. At first there was no reaction then she began to lick the lamb while making soft purring sounds.

Ruth gathered up Jock's knife and the dead lamb and rose to her feet taking the jacket with her. As she turned to distance herself from the ewe and lamb she found herself looking into the smiling face of a shepherd who was leaning on his stick in obvious appreciation of the situation.

'How long have you been here?' she said, startled.

He laughed quietly as Jock joined them. 'Long enough to see that you made a neater job of that than I could. I take it that you are a vet?'

The ewe, while still murmuring to her lamb, was getting to her feet and they moved further away with the shepherd quietly ordering his dog to follow. 'No, I'm a doctor and these are the very first lambs that ever I've delivered. But I first saw my father perform that operation on goats in Kenya and twice when I was at home and he wasn't available I had to stand in for him.'

'Well I'm very grateful to you. Even in farming there are many more pleasant jobs of a morning. You must be the Dr MacLeod that Marie speaks about. When are that pair bringing their son home so that we can judge for ourselves if he is as bonny as his granny tells us that he is?'

'Oh, you can take my word for it. He is,' Ruth laughed, then was serious. 'They don't want to build up the hopes of the grannies in case anything goes wrong with Davie's job but in the last letter I had from Elaine she said that they should be home before the end of the year.'

During the next few days there was no corner of Kintyre which Ruth didn't see. She called briefly on the Frasers and learnt that Alastair MacIntyre's aunt was still running her estate with the help of a good farm manager. She was amazed at the size of the two children. Bob Hamilton had been on the phone the previous night. He and Jackie were going to become parents.

Helen Fraser laughed. 'They intended to put off having a family for a couple of years. Jackie says that she does not know how it happened. If she doesn't know as a doctor there isn't much chance for the rest of us!'

The Friday night was spent at a production of a play called 'Johnnie Jouk the Gibbet' by the local dramatic society in which some of the cast had been pupils of Marie's.

Both Katherine and Ruth cuddled Jock when he left them on the bus for Glasgow on Saturday morning.

CHAPTER 16

In early autumn Ruth had a letter from Elaine with the news that she was expecting a spring baby.

'This one will be born in Scotland,' she wrote. 'When I was seeing practice as a student, shepherds used to tell me that a spring pup was easier to rear than an autumn one. Donald couldn't have been less trouble but both he and I are going to miss your father.'

A letter from her parents told that they also were going to miss the Sinclair family. 'But it is a comfort to us to know that you are going to gain from our loss and have them close to you. Please give our regards to Katherine and Marie and tell them that we hope that one day they will come back to Kenya. We hear that the MacLeans hope to be back here a month after Davie and Elaine are due to leave.'

As it turned out, the MacLeans visited Ruth in Edinburgh just after the Sinclairs arrived there. Despite the fact that the former had been landlords to the latter for over two years the families had never met until then. 'We'll be able to take a first hand report back to your father, not only about you, but also his adoptive grandson,' Roddy told Ruth. 'Do you think you will ever come back to Kenya to work?'

Ruth was silent for a time before answering. 'Never can be a very long word and I cannot be sure. But after living in Scotland I wouldn't go back except for some very powerful reason. As long as my parents are fit and Iain and Anna are there close to them I have no worry. Did you ask for any particular reason or just Celtic curiosity?'

Roddy laughed then was serious. 'When we left Kenya on holiday we went first to Australia. It was too hot and the flies damn near ate us. Then we went to Canada. We only caught the tail end of the Canadian winter but after living for so long in Kenya we couldn't stand the cold. We have just spent the autumn in Skye. When I was young I couldn't get away from there fast enough. Now I can't wait to get back. We haven't felt so well in years despite both having just turned sixty. I have written to Iain and told him to find a buyer for Ramasaig. We'll go back to Skye and breathe the west wind for the rest of our lives.'

Katherine Marie Sinclair was born at dawn on a beautiful spring morning. Ruth was there just in time to see her into the world but the work was done by a wee round dark haired midwife from Barra who hummed Gaelic airs throughout.

'We'll call her Kay,' said Elaine contentedly.

For Ruth the next few years passed quickly and she measured the passage of time against the progress of the Sinclair children. Many of her days off were spent with them on the beaches of the east coast, the swimming pool or just playing games in their house. But in longer breaks no chance was missed to spend time in Kintyre with Marie.

She and Jock developed a strong bond and he never tired of showing her fresh sights which were often familiar views at different times of year which brought unbelievable changes of colour. He took her to The Glen, the shepherd's house where Marie had spent most of her married life and Davie his boyhood. They walked out to the shore where Ian Boyd had found the body of Kay and then climbed to picnic at the top of Bodach na Goire from where she could almost imagine seeing America.

Shortly after arriving in Edinburgh she had taken driving lessons but had never got around to buying a car. On one visit she spoke about this to Jock. 'Just leave it wae me. Ah'll keep an eye oot.'

A month later she got a phone call. He had found a car for her. Would she come down for it or did she want him to deliver it? She could come down at the weekend. She would speak to Davie and Elaine and if they were agreeable she would bring the children with her.

Davie and Elaine left them at Glasgow and they flew down.

Jock met them at the airport with a dark green Morris 1100 which he had obviously spent some time polishing. Ruth drove with Kay strapped in a seat belt beside her. The men sat in the back. When they reached Marie's Donald became a wee boy again and he and Kay almost bowled her over before she had a chance to admire the car.

On a climb to Cnocan Lin in the early evening Ruth thought that Jock didn't look well but he brushed off her enquiry. When she got back to Edinburgh she relayed her fears to Davie and Elaine. They advised her to speak to Angus Graham who had been a surgeon in the hospital where Jock had worked during the war and who knew the wee man well. He promised to consult with Jock's GP who had been a colleague from their university days.

Two weeks later, on an evening that she would never forget, Angus Graham drove through from Glasgow to see her. He was a broad shouldered, comfortable man with a gentle brown voice which all too often had to impart bad news. Evenly he told his story. Jock Spence, witty, kind hearted wee Jock, had Carcinomatosis. He would certainly be dead in less then three months.

Although he had been expecting it and was a strong man the collapse of the tall black doctor carried him backwards before he regained his balance. He held her as sobs racked the length of her body and tears soaked the front of his shirt. Five weeks later a merciful embolism allowed Jock to die suddenly and without pain.

At the funeral a lawyer asked Davie and Ian Boyd if they could visit him the following morning. They were told that they were joint executors under the terms of a will made by Jock a month earlier. For many years he had been trading in the stock market through the investment branch of his bank. They had amassed a fortune, the major part of which was to be used for the benefit of Davie and Elaine's children. But Marie, Katherine, the Boyds, Angus Graham and Ruth were each left ten thousand pounds.

Over the next three years Ruth became isolated and lonely

amid the bustle of Edinburgh. This started with a near tragedy on the evening after Jock's funeral, when Davie's car had been involved in an accident with a lorry near Edinburgh. Wee Kay had been most seriously injured and for a time it had been feared that she would lose a leg.

Eventually she had made a complete recovery and much of the credit for this was due to an orthopaedic consultant, Archie Gillespie, a widower nearing retirement. He and Katherine became friendly, decided to get married and bought a house overlooking a sandy beach just two miles from Marie. Then Davie and Elaine were given the chance to buy the Glen farm. This they did installing a shepherd to run it. A small construction firm in Kintyre had expanded to the extent that they now needed a civil engineer and they approached Davie.

'We cannot match the salary you'll be getting at the moment. And you may have to buy your own Wellington boots,' their spokesman said.

'An offer like that is impossible to refuse,' was the reply.

Brucellosis eradication among cattle was putting pressure on the veterinary practice where Elaine had worked as a student. They offered her part time work. 'We're going to buy that old stone house in the village. I can see the top of the Glen hills from the front and the Irish coast from my kitchen.'

'Oh shut up. That's not fair when all I can see are chimney pots,' said Ruth.

'Well, we'll have to see if we can either find you a job or a husband,' Elaine told her. 'Which do you want me to look for first?'

'I've always had a job and never had a husband so I think that I should stick to the familiar,' Ruth laughed. 'Anyway you'll probably see quite a lot of me.'

'Promise,' said Elaine and embraced her quickly.

And Ruth was as good as her word. On stolen weekends she flew down and Marie picked her up at the airport but for longer visits she took her car as she enjoyed the drive.

'By Kenyan terms of distance they aren't so far away but I feel as though I've lost part of myself,' she wrote to her parents.

Christmas spent with Marie who had all the family for Christmas dinner only served to increase her unrest. 'If you cannot find a job for me soon I may have to settle for a husband' she told Elaine. 'It's getting harder and harder to go back every time I have to do it.'

Easter fell early that year and winter was reluctant to forgo its grip. For two days Marie and Ruth looked out on the driving sleet then on the third day the sun won the battle although there was still a cold north-west wind. They decided to take a car up to the Glen house then walk out on the new road that had just been completed.

'If we don't go over to the shore we'll be sheltered from the wind' said Marie. 'But if you want your cobwebs blown away we can have a wee peep from the top.'

The upper reaches of the road were still a bit rough and they had to pick their steps in places. As they climbed they became more aware of the combined noises of the wind and the crash of the sea. At that height, the force of the wind was making them keep their heads down against it, but there were only a few hundred yards of road left when a sudden blast from a car horn made them jump to the side.

A police Land Rover was just a few yards behind them. About half a mile further back an ambulance was visibly bouncing on the rough surface and much further back a blue coastguard Land Rover was making good time with two cars bringing up the rear. The police vehicle had come to a halt and men were spilling out by the time Marie and Ruth came to the end of the road. Among them was the District Officer of the local coastguard and as he was shrugging a knapsack radio onto his back he recognised Ruth and stepped hurriedly to meet her.

'There's a fishing boat in trouble and we think she could be somewhere just below. We think that at least one man is injured but the message was breaking up and we don't know how bad he is.' He nodded towards the car which was now much nearer. 'That's the local doctor's car but can you wait here in case we need you?'

As he spoke the ambulance and the other Land Rover had arrived. Men were looping coiled rope round their shoulders and some had canvas stretchers.

'Of course I'll help but my emergency bag is in my car and that's back at the Glen house.'

'We have a basic first aid kit but the doctor will have things in his car. I'm going to the top and we'll try to raise her.' He was turning to lead off his men as he spoke.

'I'll come with you' said Ruth and raised her hand to stop his protest. 'If you manage to make contact I want to know what we may be up against.'

The police sergeant turned to Marie. 'Can you wait here in case anybody else comes. If you get cold just start the engine for the heater,' he finished before hurrying after the others.

At the top the wind was so strong that it was difficult to look into it. Two of the coastguards crouched behind rocks and began to scan the sea through binoculars. After a moment one of them turned to the other. 'Just over half a mile west,' he said above the noise of the wind.

'Got her,' said the other after a pause. 'She's broached and taking a lot of water aboard but still looks to be fairly buoyant.'

'We'll try the radio,' said the District Officer crouching down beside them. Without being told, the police sergeant and another coastguard crouched and spread their oilskins to protect the microphone from the wind noise.

'Southend Coastguard calling Boy Robert. Southend Coastguard calling Boy Robert. Are you receiving us? Over.' After a silence the message was repeated but still with no result.

'Put up a flare to let them know that we're here,' he ordered. 'They may be trying to save a battery.'

There was a whoosh so close to her ear that Ruth jumped as the flare burst into a bright light above them. The radio message was repeated.

'Boy Robert calling Southend Coastguard, Boy Robert

calling Southend Coastguard. Receiving,' came a surprisingly calm voice. 'We have loss of power and are now taking in water. We have three crew uninjured but our skipper is trapped by the hand. We cannot free him. Over.'

'Southend Coastguard calling Boy Robert. Can you abandon ship? Over.'

'Boy Robert calling Southend Coastguard. Negative. We won't leave our skipper. Over.' The voice was firm.

'Southend Coastguard calling Boy Robert. We will keep in touch with you. Good luck. Over and out.'

While they had been talking the local doctor had joined them. He was dressed in a suit and a raincoat, was bareheaded and had light dress shoes on his feet. Ruth knew he was in his early sixties and no longer kept well.

'We'd better get down nearer the shore,' the officer told his men. 'We should soon know where she's likely to strike. I hope it's somewhere we can get them off before she breaks up.'

Ruth looked at the treacherously steep grassy slope dropping over a thousand feet to where the waves burst on the rocks then turned back to the elderly doctor.

'I think that I should take that,' she said as she stretched out her hand.

'I hope it has everything you may need. And thank you very much' he said as he handed over his case. Without another word he turned and scrabbled over the hill back to his car.

As his men started off with their various loads and the officer bent to lift his radio he turned to a wee smiling faced man who wasn't in uniform and had a massive coil of rope wound over his left shoulder and under his right arm.

'Do you know if anyone has the megaphone, Shorty?' he asked.'

'Dammit naw. Ah'll get it,' and he disappeared over the top at a half run.

Ruth was finding the slippery slope difficult and hadn't progressed far when the wee man caught up with her. He had a megaphone slung opposite to the rope and carried a stretcher pole.

'Swap,' he said handing her the pole and reaching to grasp the case.

Ruth looked at the burden he was already carrying. 'No, you're carrying enough as it is.'

'Och now missus. Withoot aw this Ah wid blow away in the wind. Just you use the pole the way ye wid a walkin' stick. Ah'll go in front o' ye but watch an' no stand on my heid.'

The ground fell away so steeply that there were indeed occasions when the wee man's head wasn't far from Ruth's feet. But he was expert at picking a route and she found the descent easier by following close behind him. Occasionally he paused to plot his course and Ruth kept looking out towards the boat which was now much closer. Her helper looked worried as he followed her gaze.

'She's settlin' deeper aw the time. We're goin' tae need luck. Or somethin',' he added with a glance upwards.

By the time they reached level ground the boat was wallowing sluggishly about fifty yards beyond the first of the surf. She was nearly a hundred yards from their position but every wave was bringing the water almost to their feet.

The officer pulled back a sleeve for a glance at his watch. 'The tide will still be rising for another half hour,' he said. 'There's no point in going nearer till we know exactly where she's going to ground.' Then as he turned to look out to sea again he let out a roar. 'Come back here! Where the hell do you think you're going?'

But the object of the question would never have heard it over the noise of wind and sea and the megaphone which might have helped was still slung over his shoulder. Shorty had slipped away from the main group and by the time he was noticed was halfway out in his scramble over the rocks and at times disappearing in spume.

A wave broke over him before he reached a slightly higher rock. A swirl of the tide was taking the boat slowly past him in a southerly direction although the main tide was still running north. By this time she was quite close to the man on the rock and the watchers could see three men crouched over something on the deck just forward of the hold. They saw Shorty unhitch the megaphone and could hear his voice but couldn't make out what he said. As he started to unwind the rope from his shoulder one of the fishermen scrabbled across the deck and a heaving line snaked through the air. Within seconds they saw it being pulled back with the end of Shorty's rope attached.

'What the hell's he going to do?' said the Officer. 'If he tries to make her fast out there she'll smash herself in seconds.'

A big man not in uniform shouldered his way to the front. He looked out to sea, turned to glance back to the cliffs above then back to where the wee man was straining on the rope and at times disappearing from sight again, despite his position on the rock.

'Ah ken whit he's daein',' he said explosively. 'He's tryin' tae bring her in tae the Smugglers Cut. But the wee bugger's no heavy enough. Erchie, come you wi' me. An' we could dae wi' you tae, Wullie.'

The latter was said to the police sergeant before he turned to the officer. 'Set you up over there' he commanded pointing to a large slab of rock with a sheer side leading down to the water.

The officer watched the three powerful men begin to pick their way over the rocks then, 'I thought that I was in charge here,' he said.

By the time they were in position there were four men on the rope. Slowly the bow of the wallowing hulk came round until it was almost pointing to the shore. Then they saw Shorty leave the other three keeping tension on the rope and climb to the top of the rock where he stood with his right arm upraised looking out to sea. His left arm was held with the flat of his palm towards the other three.

Suddenly his arm chopped downwards and the urge of his voice could be heard as the three fell back on the rope.

Nothing happened for a second or two then as a huge wave began to lift, the voice was again heard on the shore.

'Hing on, for god's sake hing on!' as the wave broke over the rocks and the men disappeared. The boat was carried past them. When the water receded Shorty was clinging like a limpet to his rock while the others lay in a tumbled heap below him. The next two smaller waves carried the boat forward till she grounded just below the shelf where the coast-guards stood. There was a horrible splintering sound as she shuffled on the swell.

Ruth looked to see three men getting unsteadily to their feet while a fourth was crouched against the cog wheels of the winch. She turned to the Officer. 'Can you get me down there?' she asked.

'We can,' he said 'but I'm not happy. Each wave is forcing more water into her. If she settles before the tide drops she'll be completely awash.'

'Then we'd better hurry. Can you take the other three up as soon as you lower me? After what they've been through they're in no fit state to see what I may have to do.'

When Ruth saw her patient her worst fears were confirmed. The man's palm was firmly trapped between the cogs with only the heel of the hand visible. He had obviously been in this position for some hours as any blood which hadn't been washed away was dark and congealed. As she made her examination she was conscious of a shouted argument between the coastguards and the crew who were unwilling to leave their skipper.

Her case was lowered and as she looked for a safe place to put it down there was a thump on the deck and the round, grinning face of Shorty appeared beside her. He grasped the end of the still dangling rope and turned to the three men.

'Now boys,' he said 'we havenae time tae be jawin'.' Before there was time for protest the rope was whipped round the waist of the nearest man, swiftly knotted, an urgent upward motion of his arm to the men above and the man's feet left the deck. The other two were dealt with in a similar summary fashion. Meanwhile Ruth knelt beside the man on the deck and spoke to him while she assembled a syringe. He was very pale but surprisingly composed.

'I'm going to have to amputate your hand' she told him. 'I'm going to inject an anaesthetic but I'm afraid there may still be some pain. I'm sorry there's no other way.'

'Don't worry, Doc. Up to five minutes ago I was sure we were all going to drown. Anyway if I have to lose a hand I'm glad that it has to be the left. I just hope this old tub stays in one piece long enough for you to do the job.'

As he was speaking Ruth had drawn an ampoule of sterile water into the syringe, snapped the neck of a phial of Lignocaine powder and was allowing the two to mix. His accent was unfamiliar to Ruth

'Where are you from?' she asked by way of distraction as she gently drew back his sleeve to get injection sites.

'Lossiemouth. My name's Hugh Main.'

'I'm Ruth MacLeod and I'm from Kenya but I've been in Edinburgh for the last nine years.' As she reached for scissors to cut the sleeve of the oilskin the third member of the trio, having cleared the deck, crouched on the other side..

'An Ahm Shorty. Ah've been called that for so long that Ah've forgotten ma name. An' Ah'll juist cry you Doctor, missus,' he said. 'Ah don't like cryin' doctors or ministers by their first names. Here, Ah'll dae that.' Ruth was finding the scissors inadequate to deal with the tough oilskin. Shorty rummaged in a pocket and produced a knife. Stepping in front of Hugh and leaning over he slipped two fingers under the sleeve, slid the blade of the knife between them and drawing it upwards split the sleeve to halfway up the forearm. 'My God whit dae ye sharpen that on?' said Hugh in his sing-song voice.

'The wife's tongue,' grinned Shorty as he slipped the knife back into his pocket.

The boat had been grinding with each swell but the noises were becoming louder. 'Can you swim, Shorty?' asked Hugh.

'Naw. But och, don't be worryin'. Ah'll make for the

bottom an' run like hell,' he was told.

As Ruth was starting to apply a tourniquet Shorty again reached in a pocket and held up a roll of string. 'Ham twine' he said. 'If ye show me where ye want it Ah'll put it on for ye.'

Ruth indicated three sites when she was sure that there was enough twine. 'Top yin first?' She nodded. As Ruth leaned forward to put her finger on the first knot he elbowed her away. 'Nae need,' he said shortly. The knot didn't slip.

'Ready Hugh?' she asked quietly when Shorty had finished.

'Aye,' came the reply 'noo that Ah'm tied up lake a ham.' Shorty laughed.

As Ruth reached for a scalpel he dropped to his knees behind Hugh and passed his arms round the other man's chest. 'Cuddle in son,' he said in a voice oiled by chortle. 'And close your eyes,' he added seriously. After the first incision Ruth felt Hugh's position change. The man had fainted and Shorty had him clasped to his own body. 'Carry on doctor,' the wee man said evenly. She saw that he didn't look away from what she was doing.

Mercifully Hugh was still unconscious when Shorty insisted on Ruth being first to be hauled up on to the rock. Next came Hugh then the wee man with Ruth's case clasped to his chest. By the time he had gathered himself together Hugh had been placed on a stretcher and four men were bearing it towards the steep slope.

'Haud on,' he shouted then pointed to the radio. 'Are ye in touch wi' anybody?' he asked.

'Yes. There's a boat sheltering in the lee of Rathlin. He's keeping a listening watch and can relay messages.'

'Right. Tell them tae get an ambulance tae the lighthouse. If we keep low doon we'll pick up the track fae Ballymontgomery tae the Packmans Grave. We should hit the road in little mair than half an oor.'

As they were gathering up their loads somebody pointed over the edge. The Boy Robert had disappeared.

CHAPTER 17

Three nights later Ruth was reluctantly contemplating next morning's departure for Edinburgh. The prospect was not made any more inviting by the fact that she had just enjoyed two days of beautiful spring weather and the forecast was good for the next few days. She and Marie were sitting outside watching the sun hasten to hide behind the Moil when the local doctor came round the corner to join them. He looked wearied as he sat down and Marie went off to bring him a cup of coffee. He sipped in silence until the meniscus was wiped away by the hill before he turned to Ruth.

'I've just spoken to the Southern General on the phone. Hugh Main is doing so well that he has been asking when he can go home. You did a good job. He was lucky that you went down instead of me.'

'The man who deserves a lot of the credit is Shorty. It was like having my father with me. He never gave me any cause to doubt that I could do it,. And if I hadn't been there he would just have taken out that knife of his and got on with the job on his own. He never flinched even when a spurt of blood landed on his face. There is a level of stoicism in the rural Scot that would be difficult to find even in the tribes of Africa.'

The doctor noticed that Ruth's speech was becoming faster and she was displaying little of the stoicism of which she spoke. The flow was only interrupted when he turned to face her.

'Are you feeling all right?' he asked gently.

'No, I bloody well am not. Look!' Neither Marie nor the doctor had ever heard her swear. Startled, they followed the direction of her pointing arm. The Moil hills were framed by a fiery red sky and the light of the hidden sun was lancing off the heaving Atlantic making a dramatic display in the darkening sky. After a moment or two she turned back to the doctor. The tears in her eyes were beginning to spill onto her cheeks.

'I have to go back to Edinburgh tomorrow.' Her tone was level. 'I simply don't want to go. My family are in Kenya. My friends are here. Oh yes, I know plenty of people in Edinburgh. But they are professional acquaintances rather than real friends. And wee Shorty was just the last straw. If he came as a patient with a sore foot you could tell him about your sore heart while you were treating him. As a consultant, no matter how hard you may try, you can never get really close to your patient.'

She broke off as she became conscious of a wide smile on the face of the other doctor. As she started to speak again he held up his hand.

'I wasn't sure how to approach this but you have just made it easy for me. I want to retire. We have a grandson in Canada whom we have never seen. When that has been corrected I want to come back here and sit on a riverbank with my pipe, my thoughts and a fishing rod. Would you like to take over from me? I'd be happy to recommend you.'

Ruth threw her arms round his neck in a hug which almost choked him. She applied for the post as soon as she got back to Edinburgh and then suffered a period of doubt during which she asked herself many questions. She would be setting her career on a new course. She liked her consultancy work and the buzz of a big hospital, but on many occasions she saw her patients only once. The personal touch was never given a chance to develop.

This was a community whose heart was a village. In such a community she had spent her childhood but there she had been born into the community. She was 'Juist lake the rest' as Jock would have told her. Here she would be the only black face in a white community with no other cosmopolitan elements. And, in addition to being young and black, she would be their first female doctor, probably the first black person that many would have seen.

One member of the interview panel tried to make as many difficulties as possible. He even made an attempt to humiliate her by asking a question in bad Swahili. This being a lingua franca in much of Africa Ruth understood roughly what he said but by this time she was fed up with him. Quietly, using careful Gaelic, she asked what he had said. Another man, who she was later to learn was the local schoolmaster, laughed. Although the other members seemed to be sympathetic to her Ruth was conscious that she had probably made an enemy.

Six weeks later the appointment was confirmed. She took her first surgery on the first day of July. Not only had her predecessor kept excellent records but he had added pencilled footnotes to many of the cards giving sometimes highly amusing but, in a couple of cases, disturbing hints of character traits.

Her first three patients were from the caravan park on the beach. Two were children suffering from an excess of the sun and the third was a woman who had neglected some of the basic rules of cooking in order to spend more time on the golf course and as a result found herself with a very volatile digestive system. Being a country practice the doctor combined as dispenser. Ruth gave her some pills, told her to avoid the golf course for a couple of days unless she knew where the bunkers were and she went away looking rather shocked.

Ruth was writing a note to herself to have a check of the contents of the drugs cabinet when she heard a discreet cough. She looked up to see an elderly man with his cap in his hand. He had a head of grizzled hair not unlike her father.

'Excuse me, but I was looking for the doctor.'

'I am the doctor' she said with a smile.

'Och yes indeed.' He was flustered. 'Och yes. Well I can see you're busy. I'll come back another day,' and he turned away.

Ruth rose and with three long but unhurried strides gently pushed the door closed and turned back to look at her patient. Although his clothes were old fashioned and had been some time absent from an ironing board he had obviously dressed himself for the occasion. He was wearing a dark grey suit of rough tweed with a heavy cotton shirt and tie. The heat of the day didn't seem to trouble him. His black boots shone dully.

Ruth smiled and extended her hand. 'I'm your new doctor. My name is Dr Ruth MacLeod.'

He looked her full in the face for a moment then slowly his hand came out. 'Are you the lassie that helped Shorty to take the hand off the man?'

'Yes.' Ruth kept a straight face with difficulty.

'Och yes. Well now. Och yes indeed.' And he moved to the patients' chair as Ruth went back behind her desk. Giving him time to settle, she first of all made a remark about the weather and from that went into a short discussion about the number of summer visitors. She saw that he moved uncomfortably in his chair.

'Now,' she said when he was more relaxed, 'what seems to be the trouble?'

'Och it is nothing just. Och no. Just nothing. But the last time I was here the doctor gave me some wee sweeties, just wee white sweeties. And I was wondering just, would there be any left?'

'Could you tell me your name please?'

'Och yes indeed. Archibald,' and he smiled. 'Archibald Archibald.'

'But what is your surname Archie?' Ruth was reaching to the drawer of indexed cards.

'Archibald just. I am Archibald Archibald but folks just call me Dooble Erchie.'

His card was near the front and was the only one bearing the surname. 'Can you remember when you last visited your doctor?' she asked as she was bringing it out.

'Och well now I cannot be sure, just. It's a wee while

since.' He thought for a moment. 'Now was it the time of the gale? Or was it the year of the snow? Now I just can't be sure. But I kept a few of the wee sweeties and took them a few days ago. Maybe I'd be fine if I just had a few more. Och yes.'

Ruth checked his card. The last entry had been made just over six years before.

'Och indeed,' he agreed when she told him. 'It was when Heather was just a baby. Fancy me not remembering that now.'

The date of birth on his card indicated that he was sixty eight years of age. During these exchanges Ruth formed the impression that he was trying to hide the fact he was in some pain. After a bit of reluctance he shed his jacket and loosened his shirt to let her listen to his chest. His heartbeat was strong, slow and regular. It was slightly more difficult to persuade him to lie on the couch for examination.

He was holding himself so tense that it wasn't easy to spot any reaction as she gently probed his stomach and he denied feeling any pain, but as she moved her hand to his lower abdomen she felt him flinch beneath her touch. She pressed low down on his right side and lifted her hand smartly. He groaned and his mouth clamped shut. Ruth drew the patients' chair close to the couch and sat down beside him. There was a thin film of sweat on his forehead.

'Mr Archibald, have you been sick recently?' she asked.

'A wee bittie, I was walking down. But just a bittie, I was hurrying,' he explained.

'When did you last eat anything?'

'Yesterday just. I took a cup of tea this morning. I wasn't hungry for anything else. I'll be all right in a wee whiley.' The last was said in the form of a question and, for the first time, there was a note of anxiety in his voice.

'Yes, you will,' she said with assurance. 'But I want you to go to hospital in Glasgow.'

'Glasgow! Och no I can't be doing that. I can't be leaving Heather on her own.'

Ruth was puzzled. 'Is Heather your daughter?' He laughed then gripped his side. 'No no' he said after a moment. 'Heather is my wee terrier.'

Ruth could see signs of a dangerously time-consuming argument which she didn't want to prolong and impulsively offered a solution.

'She can stay with me until you come home.' This seemed to settle his mind and he waited quietly while she phoned to arrange for an ambulance to pick him up from his house and for an air ambulance to come.

'What's wrong with me anyway, doctor?' he asked as she was driving him home. It was the first time that he had shown any curiosity about his condition.

'Well, you have a badly inflamed appendix that I think will have to come out,' she said carefully.

'Appendix. Och indeed is that all. I thought that it was maybe something serious.'

The wee cottage was neat with a well weeded shore gravel path leading to a door framed by climbing roses. From inside came the fierce barking of a dog but when the door was opened the noise ceased and a small, blond cairn terrier rushed out to greet them excitedly. Ruth noted with relief that the welcome was extended to both of them without favour. The dog shadowed Ruth as, following the old man's directions, she gathered together the essentials for the trip to hospital then sat at her feet as they waited for the ambulance. Her master noted this with contentment.

'Have you ever been in hospital before?' Ruth asked to fill a silence.

'Och yes.'

'How long ago was that?' Obviously information wasn't going to be liberally dispensed.

'Och a long time. Och yes indeed. A long time ago.' Then surprisingly he went on. 'Och yes it was in France you see. I got a wee bit knock in the trenches.' With that Heather began to growl and they became aware of the noise of the ambulance outside. The old man bent to fondle the dog's ears then looked up at Ruth. 'Thank you. Thank you very much,' he said simply.

'I'll enjoy her company. But I promise that I'll give her back to you when you come home.'

It was a reluctant Ruth who, a short two weeks later, kept her word. Because of the scattered nature of the practice and the fact that many families had no form of transport other than a bicycle, home visits were necessary for many things which, in a town, would have been dealt with in a surgery. This gave a sense of freedom which Ruth found relaxing after working in a hospital. Heather loved the car and spent her travelling time standing on the back seat with her forepaws on the back of the front passenger seat. Some of the time when Ruth was on calls she sat on the parcel tray from where she could smile to anyone who passed close to the car. Her master obviously spent much time talking to her and Ruth found herself continuing the habit. The dog would turn her head from side to side in a listening attitude and Ruth felt that it would not have been surprising if she were to start answering back. Her greatest pleasure was to romp along the beach and dash in and out of the waves with the children of the holidaymakers.

Dooble Erchie had returned from his operation slightly pale and not quite so sprightly of step but otherwise he declared himself quite fit to resume life as his own house-keeper. Ruth dropped in whenever she was in his area and if she was going further up the glen she would take Heather with her and drop her off on her way back. If the day was good and her master was showing signs of wishing to tackle garden work for which he wasn't yet fit, he was included in the expedition.

The longest of the unofficial notes left by the previous doctor concerned a young mother and her baby daughter who lived in what had been a farm cottage. The house cuddled in to the side of a hill and had a beautiful view. But to reach it by car involved driving through a burn, then negotiating a rough cart track. In his synopsis the doctor said that he thought the location had been deliberately chosen to discourage visitors and social contact.

'This poor girl is either hiding from something or trying to purge a memory,' he wrote. 'There is obviously something deeply distressing in her background but I have been completely unsuccessful in finding out what it is. And I now fear that the lack of progress of the daughter is in some measure related to the nervous condition of the mother. The most professional observation that I can leave you with is "good luck". I will be in Canada for two months. If you have made progress at all by the time I come back you will have done much better than my achievement of the past six months.'

On Ruth's first visit she had to abandon her car about a hundred yards short of the house and walk on by a tree-shaded path beside a chortling burn. The house had been visible from the car but as she walked a high bank cut it from view. Somebody had obviously made an effort to brighten the bank as there were several clumps of nasturtium and michaelmas daisies struggling for notice among the rough grass.

A brood of young sparrows were holding a mini parliament in the topmost branches of a hawthorn tree and Ruth had stopped to look and listen when a flat female voice made her jump. 'Good afternoon,' came defensively from a level above her and she turned to see a tall, unhealthily thin young woman with pale features in which there was no hint of welcome.

'Good afternoon, I wonder how much noise could they make if they were as big as seagulls.'

'What do you want?' There was no movement in either voice or gaze.

'Oh. I'm sorry. I'm Dr MacLeod your new doctor.' Ruth kept her own voice level.

'You'd better come up to the house then.'

Ruth rounded a tall flowering rhododendron to see the front of a single storey stone built house with a corrugated iron roof. The path to the door bisected a trimmed lawn and precisely in the centre of one of the squares a chubby child sat on a travelling rug.

Ruth knew from records that the mother called herself Mrs Margaret Thompson and that her daughter Jennifer was just under nineteen months of age. Ruth walked across the grass and dropped to her knees on the edge of the rug to be met by the same blank stare as she had endured from the mother.

Ruth came away with a feeling of frustration from a visit that had not been a success. The mother resisted all efforts to draw her out in conversation. The baby was clean and well nourished but even a fly landing on her nose brought absolutely no change of expression. The purpose of the call had been to give a booster jag to the baby, but Ruth kept this in reserve in order to give her a credible reason for an early follow up call.

CHAPTER 18

A week later Ruth again drove through the burn and up the bumpy road. This time she had Heather for company. Ever since her last visit the weather had been dry and warm and the burn which ran down from the house carried much less water. Mrs Thompson's greeting was less hostile but still showed no warmth but, surprisingly, she bent to present the back of her hand to Heather then gently ran practised fingers over the head and muzzle as the dog sat on her foot.

'She's lovely. Have you had her since she was a puppy?' The question was the first sign of interest that Ruth had seen in anything.

She explained as she was assembling a syringe and drawing the injection into the barrel. When she said that the locals referred to the dog as 'Heather Erchie' she thought that she detected a trace of a smile on the impassive face.

Apart from being slightly more tanned, Jennifer looked as if she hadn't even shifted position from the previous visit. As Ruth dropped to her knees, Heather moved to sit about a yard in front of the baby and began to turn her head from side to side as she did when she was being spoken to. When Ruth administered the injection the mother made no move to comfort the baby but other than a slight flinch there was no reaction from the patient.

Ruth spoke to Jennifer but the child was putting all her interest in Heather. The dog was crawling towards the baby with her head and tail moving from side to side in opposite symmetry to one another. As Ruth moved back Heather jumped forward and turned on her back with her paws in the air and her side resting on the baby's leg.

As the syringe was being packed away Margaret Thompson edged out of the narrow door with a tray containing two cups of coffee and sugar and milk. She glanced towards her daughter, saw the tableau of child and dog but placed the tray on the grass without comment.

Despite a slight heat haze the view which funnelled to the Irish coast between the two headlands was impressive and as they watched, a cruise liner appeared to cut a white arrowhead in the smooth azure of the sea. A sudden gasp from the mother tore Ruth's eyes back toward the baby. Heather had moved off to a distance of about three feet and again her twitching body was belly up and she was making short murmuring noises and Jennifer had rocked forward to her hands and knees and was crawling towards the dog.

Her movements were jerky and uncoordinated but as the dog waited patiently she made progress. When the gap was closed she flopped back on her bottom and Heather waited to have her tummy tickled. After a moment or two the dog reset the stage. This time progress was faster and Jennifer began to chortle. This was the first sound that Ruth had heard her make.

Suddenly, a wail of excruciating intensity split the gentle hum of the pollen-seeking bees. Heather shook her head and gave a short yelp of distress as the noise assaulted her sensitive ears. Ruth felt herself shiver and goose pimples appeared on her arms in reaction to the sheer agony of the sound. Margaret Thompson was sitting bolt upright with her head thrown back and the open mouthed howl seemed being torn from the very depths of her soul.

Heather backed stiff legged to stand in front of the baby and the steady obtrusion of her growls brought the wail down to juddering, breath-caught sobs as the mother collapsed against her doctor and the two rocked in a sitting position. The one person who hadn't reacted to the disturbance of the peace was Jennifer. All her attention was on the dog which, satisfied that there was no threat to the safety of her friend, had again moved away and was lying on her back in anticipation of having her tummy tickled. As she slowly regained control, words began to spill from Margaret Thompson.

At first her speech was disjointed and almost incoherent and a squeal of delight from Jennifer provoked a fresh bout of sobbing though this finally settled and the story emerged. She was a qualified vet and had met her husband when, after leaving college, she had joined a mixed practice in a small town in Yorkshire.

'I grew up in the north of Scotland. My father was a minister in the Free Church. He was a good, kind wee man but my mother was a snob and she led him a miserable life. Her people had been well off. They married when she was in her late thirties and my father was almost fifty.'

'She was desperate for the respectability of being married but didn't realise that I might be part of the bargain. She resented my father for making her pregnant. Fortunately I was a bonny child and could be shown off, but I gave her a big belly and stretch marks.'

She giggled and this made her catch her breath again but after a second or two she continued. 'I really don't know why she was so bothered about stretch marks because I'm sure that nobody, my father included, would ever see them. But to bring it up at tea parties with the young mothers of the parish made her feel like one of them.'

'I've no idea of how she ever allowed herself to become a mother in the first place. If she could have kept her legs crossed while I was being delivered I'm sure she would have done it. Daddy escaped to Heaven when I was sixteen and I was glad. It would be the first happiness the poor wee man would have known in years. Then when I was seventeen I got away to college.'

Jennifer and Heather were playing their own version of tig. The dog would allow the child to catch up, lie for a moment or two to have her tummy tickled then move off to be followed by the chortling child. In even tones the rich, brown, controlled voice continued the biography. Ruth saw that the eyes of the mother now followed every move of the child. There was light and animation in the previously impassive face. To Ruth, who was brought up in the freedom of an African village, the story was strange almost to the point of being sinister. As a child Margaret Thompson was never allowed the company of boys as playmates and her mother had instilled fear of men in her young mind.

'Daddy was never allowed to bath me or put me to bed. If he came into a room when I was being dressed my mother covered me up until he left. I never even saw my father stripped to the waist and now I can vaguely remember wondering why women bulged at the front and men didn't.'

'But she couldn't prevent me going to school. It was a lovely one-teacher country school but the toilet arrangements were rather primitive. One day I saw one of the boys have a pee and I couldn't understand how he did it. I tried for days to do the same and wet my pants in the process. Fortunately our teacher was both young and sensible. One Friday afternoon in each month was set aside for what she called her girls class. The boys were sent out to play football or shinty. The younger children got out an hour earlier than the older classes. She explained puberty and growing up to the older girls and took the fear away.'

High school had been fun as she left home in the early morning and wasn't home until the evening. But her father was becoming increasingly unwell and then died quite suddenly just at the end of her fifth year.

'It was just at the end of June.' Her voice was now level and controlled and the tears seemed exhausted. 'I thought that it was so unfair. In a way I was glad for him because I was sure that he would be happier in death than ever he could have been since marrying my mother. But if he had even lived for another month I would have been there to care for him.'

A deep sob rasped its way from her throat with a suddenness which startled Ruth. After a moment of silence control returned and she was able to go on.

'There was a hill behind the manse and Daddy and I used to go up there to watch the sunset. In the summer swallows nested in the eaves and the parent birds would fly over us collecting insects to feed their young. I went there every night during that summer holiday and then went to bed to cry myself to sleep. I never saw my mother shed a tear.'

After a rather miserable year she got away to vet college in Edinburgh. There she found that the other girls on her course were wary of her when they heard that she was a daughter of the manse. But not so the boys. This tall, unworldly girl, who kept herself to herself became a trophy to be captured. 'At first I was flattered. Some of them had cars and I was taken for runs in the country. Some of them hadn't and it was visits to the pictures and sometimes the theatre. But no matter. None of them got beyond a second date without a hand on my knee. In the end I became known as the Ice Maiden and sometimes Virgin Meg.'

She was three months in practice when her mother died. Although there had been little parental bond she suddenly felt as though she was alone in the world. One of the vets, a man some ten years older, was very good to her. He started to take her out but never tried to take advantage. He bought her a West Highland terrier and they used to take it for walks on the Yorkshire moors. Still he behaved as the perfect gentleman.

'Then one day we had taken a picnic. I was so damned naive that I didn't realise what was happening. And then I was looking up at the sky and this man's head was between me and it. I had heard stories but chosen to disregard them.'

Six weeks later she realised she was pregnant. The senior partner of the firm was a family man and very proud of his own children.

'If this man hadn't married me he would probably have been sacked. He was mid thirties and had never been anything more than an assistant. He had moved around a lot and could have found it difficult to get another job.

After they were married he stayed out late at night and there were many phone calls which she was sure were not professional. Then the night of the birth of the baby he still wasn't home and she had to get a neighbour to take her to the maternity hospital. Even after the baby was born he still hadn't appeared. Then, early on the dark winter morning her doctor came back to see her accompanied by a policewoman. Her husband had been killed in a car crash. At first she felt numb, then sad. But two days later this was replaced by bitter anger.

'He had the nurse from the veterinary practice in the car with him and she was also killed and she was four months pregnant with his baby. Hamish, my wee dog, had been with them and thrown out when the car turned over. He ran into the path of another car and was so badly injured that he had to be put down. I had fed Jennifer myself for the first two days. Then I couldn't make myself do it.'

The final irony had been when three other women from different parts of the country had brought paternity suits against her husband's estate.

'I felt a mixture of guilt and stupidity. I just couldn't give love to his baby. I fed her and clothed her but have hardly spoken to her and never played with her. It wasn't until I saw her playing with Heather that I realised that what I was doing was nothing short of neglect.'

The dog was licking the child's bare feet and Jennifer was squealing with delight. Ruth slid herself closer to Margaret. 'Heather, come here' she commanded. The dog stood, hesitated for a moment, then slowly walked forward and flopped between the two women. Jennifer looked, then tumbled forward to her hands and knees and started to crawl forward in pursuit. When she was close her mother bent forward, lifted her into her arms and her daughter snuggled against her neck.

Despite a wet, miserable day Ruth's next visit to Gartbeg found a bright cheery house. She could hear Margaret singing as she approached the door and paused to enjoy the mellifluous sound of 'All through the night' being treated to a rich contralto voice. She had made a detour to pick up Heather and had explained to Dooble Erchie the reason for wanting to take her.

'Leave her wi' the wean for a couple o' days if ye think

it'll dae good' he offered.

Ruth knew the generosity of the offer as his pet was his only real company. She explained that taking Heather to visit rather than leaving her to stay not only gave Jennifer something to look forward to but also provided an excuse for herself to visit.

'Ach weel, ye'll ken best yersel' he said but the relief was evident in his voice.

When Ruth went into the living room of the but and ben cottage Jennifer was standing clinging to a chair. Heather shook the raindrops from her coat as she came through the door. When the child saw the dog she squealed, turned from the chair, lost her balance then squealed again as her bare bottom hit the cold stone floor. Her mother had been writing a letter at a small table and she rose, smiling, to embrace the tall black doctor.

'I'm just writing to the estate to ask if we can buy this place. It needs some money spent on it but it's such a lovely situation that I feel it would be well worth it' she told a surprised Ruth.

'Who is your laird here?' she asked.

'It's the local Estate but the old lady who owned it died soon after we came here. At present it's being looked after by trustees until the new laird comes from somewhere abroad. I think he is a nephew. She herself never married, sensible woman.' Ruth noticed the last two words were said with more humour than bitterness.

'Have you ever met the nephew?' A suspicion was stirring at the back of Ruth's mind.

'No I haven't. But I did hear that he was rather dishy.'

Ruth laughed. 'Yes, that does sound a bit like the man I was thinking of.' She went on to explain about Alastair MacIntyre from Kenya. 'He did tell me that the estate was close to the Fraser's place but in African terms twenty odd miles isn't far. He's a kindly big lad and should make a very good laird.'

As Ruth and Heather were preparing to leave a shepherd was bringing a gather of sheep through a hill gate just above the house. Ruth had carried Jennifer to the door but had then set her down and was holding her by the hand while the child had her other hand on Heather's collar. The man had opened the gate and two dogs were doing the work of hustling the sheep down towards the rough road. The main flock drew cleanly onto the track but a few of the stragglers found a gap in the hedge and set off across the field.

One of the dogs had already gone ahead to slow the progress of the main bunch. At a sharp command the other leapt the burn but as it was clearing the undergrowth there was a crisp, twig snapping crack. The dog fell over, tried to rise, then collapsed again with its tongue going to its right hind leg. Margaret ran forward, jumped from the edge of the bank to the road, then passed the shepherd to round the top of the hedge. When she neared the dog she slowed before dropping to her knees beside it.

After a moment she climbed to her feet. One hand had a firm grasp of the dog by the nape of the neck and the other arm was under its body.

Ordering Heather to wait with Jennifer, Ruth came down and the two met beside the shepherd. The right hind leg of the dog dangled from mid thigh.

'What have you got in your bag?' asked Margaret.

'Nothing for a general anaesthetic but I've got Lignocaine and plaster bandage.'

'Perfect. Can you spare another half hour or so?'

After a nod from the doctor she turned to the shepherd. He was gently stroking the dog's head in front of her hand and tears glistened in his eyes. 'Can you leave him with me?' she asked. Then, as he hesitated, she went on,

'I'm a vet. I'll repair the fracture and put the leg in plaster. If you come back in the evening he'll be ready to hop home with you.' Then, as she glanced up to the door of her house she added 'Is he as good natured with children as he is with adults?'

The shepherd followed her glance. 'Is that Heather Erchie?' he asked.

'Yes.'

'That's fine. He knows her. They're pals. You can trust him with children but he can be a bit short tempered with other dogs. He had a rough time as a pup and has been evening the score ever since.'

He smiled for the first time and the girls saw he was a very handsome young man. He hooked his crook over his arm, placed a hand on each side of the dog's head and bent to look into his eyes. 'Now you behave yourself Roy' he said then turned abruptly away.

Heather was left to play with Jennifer in the living room and Roy was deposited on a sheet which Ruth had thrown over Margaret's bed. Then Ruth was left to hold the dog as the vet took over.

'Would you like me to muzzle him?'

'No. Our dogs at home often picked up injuries and Dad taught me how to hold them when he had to treat them.'

Margaret produced a bag from a cupboard. 'I still have my instruments but no drugs' she said.

Carefully the leg hair was clipped while the injection took effect. Then, after a gentle finger exploration, a grunt of satisfaction and the bandage was applied. Throughout, the dog had given no signal of distress.

'Do you know the shepherd?' asked Margaret as they waited for the plaster to harden. 'He seemed very upset about his dog.'

Ruth was quiet for a moment. 'I think that I've just worked out who he is,' she said eventually. 'Marie was teasing me about this handsome young shepherd but until today I hadn't met him. Now I can see what she meant. He's a widower and has a wee boy of four. His mother-in-law lives with him and she brought her grandson to see me just last week. The child told me about his dog Roy so this must be him.'

She had been speaking with a gently restraining hand on the dog's shoulder and at the mention of his name the dog turned his head and began to lick her wrist.

CHAPTER 19

For the first couple of months after taking up her post Ruth lived in a farm cottage. It was in a beautiful situation surrounded by grazing cattle and green fields but she found it lonely, particularly when returning from night time call outs. Consequently she was glad that renovations to the doctor's house in the centre of the village were completed before the onset of winter.

To furnish a three bedroom house which also had two large bow windowed public rooms was going to be a considerable exercise. Fortunately money wasn't a problem. She had consulted the bank which had handled Jock's affairs and they were now successfully investing her legacy. Marie had a suggestion. 'Why don't you involve Margaret Thompson? I can look after Jennifer.'

Margaret's response was enthusiastic and her skills surprising to Ruth. Her own house furnishings barely exceeded spartan level but it soon became apparent that this was more due to state of mind than ability or taste. She arrived with a sketch pad. 'This is going to be costly,' she said with mock seriousness.

'But I'm wealthy.'

'Boy oh boy, this is going to be fun,' and Ruth found herself in a bear hug. 'Now, we'll start at the rafters and work our way out to the doorstep.' As Ruth followed with echoing footsteps on the bare wood of the staircase she marvelled at the change wrought on her companion by a few short weeks. Two days later, after a quiet morning surgery, they bore their ideas to the delighted owner of the furniture store in the town. While they considered bedrooms, one of which was bigger than the other two and had a beautiful view over the golf course to Dunaverty and the sea, Margaret had made only the minimum of comments and noted and sketched as Ruth spoke. But when they finished and came out to the top hall she marched straight to the head of the stairs and plumped down to sit on the second highest step.

'Now,' she said as she looked at the rich dark oak of the banisters before going on with a catch in her voice, 'this is beautiful.' And after another pause 'The stairway in the manse where I was born was like this but my mother was so bloody virginal that she had it painted white. Can you imagine how anyone could do that? It was sheer bloody vandalism.'

Her face was flushed as she turned to Ruth. 'This wood will be fed just to let it know that it is loved. There will be a rich wine coloured carpet. The wallpaper will be plain and there,' she indicated the flat face of the stairwell 'you are going to have a mural which I will paint for you of your favourite view.'

Ruth laughed. 'Am I allowed a person in the mural?'

'No. Have him in your heart but not on your wall. It saves explanation if you change your mind.'

Then she put her hand to her mouth and reached for the sketch pad with the other.

'I'm sorry. I forgot that this is your house. What would you like here?'

'I want exactly as you described it and I know just the view which I want for the mural. But how did you know that the person would have been a man?'

'Pal,' came the cryptic answer 'that is just another field which, until a few weeks ago, I didn't even know had an entrance gate.'

At the end of three busy weeks the job was complete. On her first morning in residence Ruth came downstairs in her dressing gown to switch on the kettle. She opened all the curtains and stood at each window, to look over the September garden to the view beyond and moved to the farmer who was gathering sheep for market from the field on the other side of the road, then bore her cup of tea to the top step of the stair and sat to enjoy the mural. The scene was copied from a photograph which she had taken just a week before Jock's death.

It had shown the wee man standing at the top of Cnocan Lin and she remembered the fun they had had trying to position him so that she could bring the view into the photograph without his features being shadowed by the westering sun. It had been a beautiful day in early autumn and the soft blue of the Irish coast had been clearly visible.

Margaret had worked steadily for four days. In the foreground she had replaced Jock with a roe deer stag. She had depicted him standing looking out of the picture with a forefoot raised ready for fight or flight. In the background beyond the cow dotted green of the fields, she had caught the crystalline flashes of the sun on the sea. Ruth found it easy to remember her advice to keep the man in her heart and tears of mixed joy and sorrow splashed the front of her dressing gown.

The clattering ring of the telephone brought her back to being a doctor who was urgently needed. There had been a tractor accident on a nearby farm. The farmer, a young man, had jumped off a tractor while it was still moving, slipped, and the rear wheel had gone over his leg and shattered the shinbone. By the time Ruth got there she was preceded by the next door neighbour who looked nearly as shocked as the victim. It was pointless to waste time on examination beyond a cursory glance at the protruding bone. The man's wife was standing with a painfully sobbing wee girl clinging to her legs.

'I'm sending you to Glasgow to get that fixed,' Ruth told her patient. 'I'll go and phone for an ambulance and arrange for the air ambulance then we'll try to make you as comfortable as possible for travelling.'

'But I can't go to Glasgow,' the protest came through the gritted teeth of pain. 'There's only ourselves here. Can you not put it in plaster?'

'If I did and you tried to carry on working you would almost certainly be lame for the rest of your life and could even lose your leg. This way you'll be as good as new in a few weeks.' She moved back close to him and lifted the hem of her skirt. 'Give me your hand,' she commanded. She guided his hand to just below her knee. 'Now' she said 'feel down the bone and tell me if you can find a join.'

Gently he moved his hand down and up then repeated the manoeuvre more firmly. 'No,' he said. 'Should I?'

'Only because I suffered a similar fracture to yours. I was taken overnight in the back of a truck to get me to a main hospital. It wasn't nice at the time but I've been grateful ever since.'

'Okay, Doctor, you win.' Suddenly he grinned as he looked up and Ruth realised that she was still holding her raised skirt. 'Do you think that they might give me a pair of legs like yours while they are at it?'

At the end of a day when she had lost a fight with cancer over a patient who, although elderly and in pain, had never lost sense of humour, Ruth decided to visit Margaret and Jennifer. They had seen her car cross the burn and the latter met her at the door and stretched up her hands to be lifted. With a triumphant gleam in her eyes her mother produced a letter for Ruth to read. It was from the Estate office agreeing to sell Gartbeg cottage and was signed by Alastair MacIntyre. To Ruth the asking price seemed reasonable. The signature proved her guess as to the identity of the laird.

'I take it that you can cope with this,' she said.

'Easily. My husband had taken out a hefty insurance policy not long before he died. And because he was killed in an accident the payment was doubled. I wondered why he had done so until the agent came to see me. She was young and pretty so it is a safe assumption that his motives weren't entirely altruistic. Added to this, the practice carried an insurance which pays me the equivalent of half his salary. This is linked to inflation. And even if I remarry it goes on.'

While Ruth had been sitting with Jennifer on her knee Margaret had been preparing coffee.

'Now then young lady,' she said as she brought a steaming

mug 'you run through to the bedroom to play while Aunt Ruth has her coffee.'

Jennifer slipped down, toddled to the door, then turned 'Bye bye' she waved before she disappeared.

Ruth looked round what was a fairly spacious room. There were windows in the two opposite walls and though these were small there was a surprising amount of light. Further floor space was provided by an alcove which would have contained the built-in bed which would have been the cosy, night time nest of successive parents. She wondered how many children had been conceived, born and suckled in that very space.

Margaret, who had been following her gaze, turned suddenly towards her and in a split second before she spoke Ruth noticed that her face seemed to be carrying a blush.

'Ruth, can I have the pill?' she burst out.

The interruption to her train of thought was so unexpected that Ruth, who had been taking a sip of her coffee, splattered the front of her skirt. When she had caught her breath and restored some order to her person she found that Margaret hadn't followed her request with the laugh which she had expected.

'You're not pulling my leg.' Despite herself she couldn't keep the surprise from her voice.

'I'm not even sure myself.' This was said slowly.

'You remember when we set the broken leg on James Mackay's dog?' At Ruth's nod she continued. 'When he came to pick Roy up that evening Jennifer was in bed and we sat talking. I liked him. He told me about his wife's illness and his young son and I found myself telling most of my own life story. Then when he brought Roy back to have the plaster removed he had the boy with him. Hamish and Jennifer had a great time.'

She paused to take a sip of coffee. 'He now drops in once or twice a week. Sometimes he's on his own but if he can make it before Jennifer's bedtime he brings Hamish. He has never as much as laid a finger on me but when I hear him at the door I tremble like a school girl. I know how an alcoholic must feel when he looks at a whisky bottle. James is a gentleman but there are times when my only ladylike feelings are those of a lady of the night. I thought that my husband had successfully vaccinated me against such emotions. Now I'm afraid that at some point I may lose control and I know enough to realise that a red blooded man has little defence in such a situation.'

'So, Dr MacLeod, I need your professional advice but I would also greatly value your honest-to-God opinion. Am I right to be lowering the portcullis against an enemy who may never attack? And is it just possible that I am nothing more than a closet harlot?'

Ruth laughed, 'Okay. Professional advice first. I'll take your blood pressure but, subject to that there is no medical reason why you shouldn't have the pill. I have always been a believer in preventive medicine but I am not particularly well qualified to answer the rest. It wasn't until Jock died that I realised that I had probably been in love with him despite the age difference. But because he had treated me like a daughter the thought of sex never really surfaced. Tell me, would you marry this man?'

'Six months ago I would have laughed at the very idea. But, yes, I'll marry him if he ever asks me.'

Ruth considered for a moment then 'I think you are being much too hard on yourself' she said. 'You're right in your assessment of James MacKay as a gentleman. It isn't breaking any secret to tell you that his mother-in-law told me how he looked after her daughter through her illness. Now that is a source from which a man seldom enjoys praise. And I am certain that he has picked up on the vibes from how you feel about him. If men weren't sensitive to such things the human race would have become extinct centuries ago.'

'The poor man has a triple problem. His mother-in-law would like to get back to her own house. Therefore he needs a wife but also he needs a mother for his son. This is a strong man. Self imposed restraints are normally emotional in a woman and sexual in a man. James is battling with both. I feel that when he decides you won't be left in doubt.' Then she laughed. 'And don't forget to take the tablets.'

When Ruth was standing outside the door with Margaret and Jennifer a light aircraft passed low overhead. Then it turned to come round again and banked so that the pilot could wave before it continued westward.

'Who on earth could that be?' Ruth wondered.

'I think it may be the laird,' Margaret told her. 'James said that he had a pilot's licence and was hoping to buy a plane. Didn't you say that you knew him?'

'I know him very well. We were at school together and he once saved me from a very bad situation. I just couldn't see his features with the sun on the cockpit glass.'

A few days later Alastair came to see her on his way to the local Post Office. Apart from more waistline and slightly more forehead he hadn't changed.

'If ever you are meaning to go to Glasgow let me know,' he told her. 'My aunt had business interests there and having the plane saves me a lot of time. I can easily give you a lift.'

CHAPTER 20

Because the previous doctor had been so long in the area Ruth expected that it might take some time for the older patients to be comfortable with a successor who was young, black and female. Luckily, because of her friendship with the Sinclairs, she was a kent face and she knew that she had special ambassadors among the regulars in each of the local bars in Shorty and Dooble Erchie. The local schoolmaster, who was from Lewis, and intrigued by the fact that she had a knowledge of Gaelic, had asked her to give a talk to the children on a Friday afternoon.

His motive had been to encourage the brighter of his charges to seek a university education but as she told her story he realised that the missionaries who had brought up her parents had been relatives of his own and he told this to his pupils. Everyone was friendly and she felt that she had become accepted within the community.

The original village had been a row of low stone built houses with thatched roofs which had been replaced with corrugated iron. Spray of salt sea mist had shortened the life of the roofs and as they began to leak, the houses, which were little more than hovels, were demolished. Their replacement was a group of attractive semi-detached cottage houses which were built on a raised site at the other end of the village. Around the turn of the century the doctor's house had been built between these two sites and several farmers and businessmen had added similar stone houses as retirement homes. In one of these, along with his daughter-in-law and a grandson of under school age, lived the retired colonel who had been opposed to her at her interview. Ruth had met him several times while out walking but on the times when he had returned her greeting he had been brusque to the point of rudeness. On the other hand his daughter-in-law had always been pleasant. Marie had told Ruth that her husband had been killed in an army exercise which had gone wrong and that her father-in-law's irascibility made life difficult for her and her child.

The colonel was the one person in the parish who, whenever she met him, always set her wondering as to how he would react if ever she had to treat him. It wasn't with a great deal of surprise that she received a telephone call from her predecessor who had returned from his travels.

'I've just had a phone call from Colonel Paterson,' he told her. 'He tells me that his grandson has got measles. He wasn't too pleased when I insisted that I was retired but this sort of thing has to be stamped on with the heel of a navvy's boot. Since it's only a couple of doors away could you pop round and have a look. When I see what you have done with Margaret Thompson this old fool should be easy to handle.'

But when the colonel himself answered her knock at the door she realised that this wasn't going to be the case. 'What do you want?' he demanded.

'I've come to see your grandson. Dr Marshall phoned me.' She kept her voice even and inoffensive.

'Well he had no right to and we don't need you.'

Just then came the sound of a painfully retching child. Ruth shouldered the man aside and strode into the sitting room where a single bed had been set up. The young mother sat holding a bowl to the son. The child looked hot and fevered and his hands and forearms were blemished by red blotches. The retching stopped and the mother settled the child back on the pillows. There was some sick on the otherwise immaculate bed covers. Ruth pressed a thumb on one of the blotches then, when she released it, her heart turned over. The angry red colour was still there and hadn't faded at all.

'How long has he been sick like this?' she asked.

'That was the first time that he has actually been sick' said the mother. 'But he has been complaining of feeling sick. It is just measles?' she questioned anxiously. The boy had lain back exhausted and closed his eyes. Ruth nodded towards the door where the grandfather stood with a thunderous expression on his face. As the two women passed him he glanced again at the bed then followed them across the hall to the kitchen. Ruth addressed the mother.

'Mrs Paterson, I want to move your son to hospital as quickly as I can arrange it.'

'It's more serious than measles, isn't it?' There was an obvious attempt to keep her voice under control.

'Yes I'm afraid so. Your son has meningitis.' At the mother's gasp she added quickly 'I'm going to give him an immediate injection of penicillin to try to curb the inflammation. Then, rather than wait for an air ambulance, I'm going to phone a friend in the hope that he can fly us to Glasgow.'

She had been assembling and loading a syringe at the kitchen table as she spoke but when she turned to go back to the bedroom she found her way barred by a furious grand-father.

'Stupid black bitch!' he burst out. 'All this fuss over a simple case of measles. I insist that you get Marshall here and stop all this nonsense.'

Ruth drew herself to her full height to discover that she was almost two inches taller than the slipper footed man who was facing her.

'Colonel Paterson' she said coldly 'your opinion on my canine proclivities or even that I could be piebald are of little interest to me. What is important is that the time that you are forcing me to waste could cost the life of your innocent grandson. Now,' she went on rapidly and forcefully, 'while I am giving this injection you will find the telephone number for the Estate office. And,' she added as he still stood his ground 'if you don't move out of my road this instant I am going to kick you very hard in the balls.'

As she had hoped, this shocked him sufficiently for him to take a step backwards and she was able to hurry through to her patient, closely followed by his mother. When she got back to the hall the old man was speaking on the phone but replaced the receiver when he heard her coming. The Estate number was written on a telephone pad and to her relief Alastair MacIntyre answered the phone. Swiftly she explained where she was and what she wanted.

'Right,' he said without waste of time. 'How many passengers?'

'Three. The mother, myself and the child.'

'Okay. It will be easier if I fly to you. Can you look out and tell me if there's any stock on that field opposite you?'

After a quick look she told him that the field was clear. 'Fine. I've just been servicing the plane so she's ready to go. Arrange for an ambulance at the Glasgow end for an hour and a quarter from now.' He rang off.

Swiftly she made the call to the hospital before going back to check on her patient. Mary Paterson had gone to pack a case and the colonel sat on a chair by the head of the bed. His head was in his hands and tears trickled through his fingers. His grandson appeared to be asleep but his breathing was regular.

'What are the chances?' The voice was old and hesitant.

Ruth thought before she answered. 'Alastair MacIntyre has just swung the odds in our favour.'

An urgent rap made her hurry to the door. A slightly breathless Shorty stood on the step. He was carrying a frame stretcher of the type used in mountain rescue. In his other hand was a coiled heaving line.

'Shorty. Where did you come from?'

He jerked his head towards the hill and the glen beyond it. 'Big Dunlop's lassie phoned an' I just happened tae be in the Station.' He looked back along the road with a grin. 'Them young fellas are badly oot o' trainin'.'

Ruth followed his glance to see two uniformed coastguards running towards her. The faint noise of an engine could just be heard.

'That'll be the big fella comin',' said Shorty as he moved into the hall. 'We'd better be gettin' soartit oot.'

Shorty now took charge. Mary Paterson was sent for three

pillows, a bolster and a quilt or the heaviest blanket she could produce. Two of the pillows were placed against the frame on either side of the stretcher and the bolster was placed between them. The blanket was then folded in half before being pressed down to the bolster and the third pillow tucked in so that it was enclosed by the blanket. The wee man seemed satisfied then he looked up at Ruth. Noises from outside indicated that the plane had landed and was starting to taxi back towards them.

'Can ye tell me whits wrang wi' him, Doctor?'

'Meningitis.'

'Oh. Dammit that's no sae good. Poor wee Jockie.'

Then he looked up at Mary. 'Missus, can ye get me a big hankie? An' a swanky coloured yin if ye huv it?' he asked before moving to where the grandfather could be heard talking to his grandson. Shorty sat down gently on the edge of the bed. 'Hullo wee Jockie.'

'Hi, Long John,' came back with a weak smile in what was obviously an established ritual.

'John, that's rude' said his mother who had just come back.

'Och naw it's not' said Shorty. 'He's the only man in the village that Ah can look doon at.'

'Now young man.' He took a large spotted handkerchief from Mary. 'Ah'm gaun tae kidnap ye an' Ah'll huv tae blindfold ye so that ye canna see who ma' accomplices ur.'

'Shorty, you're silly,' the voice was stronger as he responded to the banter. 'I know that your accomplices are Mummy and the doctor.'

'Och so ye dae. But don't you be tellin' anybody or Ah'll huv tae gag ye as well.'

Gently but swiftly the boy was wrapped in a blanket and transferred to the stretcher. The handkerchief was laid over his eyes and the ends tucked in behind his neck before the heavy blanket was folded over and firmly tucked in. The whole operation hadn't spanned much more than a minute. Shorty grunted his satisfaction then 'How's the heid?' The question was softly asked but the reply was strong. 'Not nearly

148

as sore as it was.'

As the stretcher was borne out by the two coastguards Ruth suddenly turned back. 'I forgot to ask Dr Marshall to cover for me' she said as she went to the phone. But the colonel stopped her. 'There's no need unless you have any special instructions. I phoned him while you were giving John his injection. He chewed me up. I didn't know until today that he had been a brigadier. I suppose that a strong man doesn't need the prop of rank. Just look at wee Shorty. Dr Marshall told me to tell you that he will cover for as long as you need. And that is to include a sleep after you get back. I'm sorry. I completely forgot.'

When Ruth reached the plane Shorty had produced his heaving line from inside his jacket and was lashing down the stretcher. John had the handkerchief over his eyes but his teeth could be seen in a smile from something which had been said.

'Shorty, do you take a length of rope to bed with you at night?' asked Ruth.

'Och naw. Juist the wife.'

Mary Paterson laughed for the first time that day. But less than two minutes after take off there was little cause to be cheerful. Because of wind direction they had to take off towards the south. Half a mile on was a headland with steep cliffs dropping down to the sea. As Alastair banked to avoid this the plane hit an air pocket. There was a horrible sideways slipping motion as the plane dropped, a furious rattle of engine noise off the cliffs as the pilot increased power, and John began to be sick.

Both women lost their balance as they threw off seat belts and sprang to their feet. Ruth managed to stay upright by grabbing the frame of the stretcher and she fully tested Shorty's handiwork, but Mary slithered back beneath the seat which she had just left. John gave a cry of pain as Ruth sat him up but the bout of sickness was short lived.

'Is your head sore?' she asked as she settled him down.

'Bloody sore,' he said unexpectedly and this brought 'John

you mustn't say that,' from his mother who had regained her feet.

'Well, it is,' he defended.

The aircraft was now flying level over the sea and the noise level in the cabin was surprisingly low. Alastair had been following events behind him in a mirror above his head and when order was restored he signalled Ruth to come forward.

'How's the patient?' were his first words.

'Surprisingly good,' she told him. 'I gave him a fairly hefty injection and this seems to have stabilised him. Also, he's quite a spunky wee character and this helps no end.'

'The mother's some looker, isn't she?'

'You keep your mind on the job, boy.'

He laughed then was serious. 'I'm going to stay over the sea except for the last few minutes. That way we can fly at a low level and should avoid any more air pockets. They're giving us priority landing at the airport so there should be no time wasted.'

'How did you manage to arrange all this in so short a time? It can't be more than three quarters of an hour since I phoned you.'

'The most valuable of my various inheritances from my aunt was her secretary. I just couldn't cope without her. As a bonus, she was a controller with W.A.A.F. during the war and knows all the shortcuts.'

Ruth was pleased to see that young John had settled and was giving no signs of distress but as she turned from the stretcher her eye was drawn to the leg of his mother's trousers. There was a tear in the cloth but the worrying thing was a spreading stain on her thigh.

'I felt a sting as I was sliding but never thought too much about it.'

'Have you another pair of trousers in your bag?'

'Yes I have.'

'Well, better slip these off and let me have a look at the cut.,' Then as she spoke she glanced at Alastair's mirror.

'It's all right' said Mary. 'I didn't get a four year old boy without a man seeing my legs. Anyway I'm quite proud of them.'

As Mary straightened with her trousers in her hand she caught Alastair's eye in the mirror. He winked. She gave him a bow and both he and Ruth laughed as she leant on the seat to let the doctor examine her wound. There was a two inch vertical cut which was still issuing blood.

'This should really be stitched but I'll draw it together with a dressing meantime. Let somebody see it when you get to the hospital.'

As Mary dressed, Ruth leant over John and his fingers found her wrist. He brought his other hand up to his face and eased the handkerchief down from one eye. 'Keek,' he said and gave a chortle. Then, almost immediately, 'I'm going to be sick again.'

Ruth sat him up but there was little left in his stomach and his sickness was confined to painful retching which made him hold his head. When it was over he lay back white faced and exhausted with a film of sweat on his face. It was with intense relief that both women picked up the signal from their pilot to fasten seat belts for landing. As they approached Alastair was talking into his headset and as the plane slowed on the runway a small van with a flashing yellow light accelerated past them and led them to the edge of the airfield where an ambulance stood, attended by two uniformed men and an emergency team of a doctor and a nurse.

By the time the plane door opened, Ruth and Mary had undone Shorty's handiwork and the ambulance team took over. Their movements appeared unhurried but Ruth had barely time to speak to the doctor, hand over her notes and receive a quick hug from a tearful Mary Paterson before the wailing siren split the traffic. Ruth's shoulders began to shake with sobs and she turned to find herself folded to the broad chest of Alastair.

'I know that it's foolish to get emotionally involved,' she said when she had regained control of her voice. 'But that bright wee boy has so much to give the world. And his mother has already lost so much.' She leant back to look into the eyes of this big man who was only a couple of inches taller than herself. 'If his bloody old grandfather ever needs an enema I'll be the first volunteer to do the job,' she said explosively.

Alastair decided to wait before asking for permission to take off in order to let any backlog caused by their arrival to be cleared. They went to the terminal building for a snack. Alastair phoned his office and Ruth phoned Dr Marshall to learn that he was coping adequately on a quiet day.

'Get a good night's sleep. I'll take all phone calls until surgery time tomorrow.'

After they had their meal they sat talking comfortably until Ruth glanced at her watch.

'Alastair, can you land that thing in the dark? she asked anxiously.

'Yes, but it's time that we were making a move. As yet I'm not all that happy about night flying. But do you want to give the hospital a ring before we leave?'

The nurse who answered the phone was sparing with information but when Ruth explained that she was the child's GP she offered to let her speak to a doctor. A modulated male voice told her that her patient was very ill.

'It's a great pity that you weren't called in earlier. But I gather that isn't the mother's fault. Apart from John we have a bit of a lull and I've spent the last half hour talking to her. If her son survives she says that it will be because you moved so quickly. I agree with her. Win or lose you've certainly done your best.' Then his voice changed to a lighter note as he went on, 'but I would have expected no less of a London graduate of 1956. I'm George MacKenzie. I was in your year. You may remember I had a desperate crush on your pal Jackie Murray.'

Ruth recalled a tall bespectacled serious young man who was reputed to be from very wealthy Scottish parents. 'Of course I remember you, George. How long have you been in Glasgow?'

'Too bloody long.' This was said with feeling. 'I've done

surgery and would like to get back to it again. Can we meet some time for a blether?'

The sun was well to the west as they sat waiting to be cleared for take off. Once airborne Ruth unclipped her seat belt and leant forward so that they could talk. As they neared the north tip of Arran Alastair began to pay more attention to his flying and began looking carefully to his right. Ruth had an anxious moment before he explained. 'I'm going to fly down the east coast of the island. Just keep your eye on the peaks. If I do a good job you'll see why.'

Over the low hills of Kintyre they could see the sun sinking to the sea beyond Islay. Opposite the Cock of Arran Alastair increased height slightly and Ruth saw a herd of deer silhouetted on the skyline. Then the fiery red of the setting sun was lancing through the peaks around Goat Fell and reflecting off the windows of the aircraft like a firework display that was blinding in intensity.

Alastair turned in his seat to grin to her. 'The fellow who sold me the plane took me down here on a test flight. It was earlier in the year and the sun was setting further north. He knew what he was doing. I bought his plane that evening.'

It was when they swung in from the sea that Ruth realised how quickly the light was fading. Alastair circled low above a large stone built house and a row of lights appeared in a field.

'My secretary lives in the house and she would have been listening for us. The lights are controlled from her office. The wife of one of my shepherds comes in every week day to attend to cooking and housework. I'm the best looked after man in the country.'

'Now,' he added when the plane was lashed down, 'do you really need to go home tonight?'

'It isn't essential. Dr Marshall is taking all calls.'

'Good. When I was on the phone I asked the ladies to make up a bed for you. And I'll guarantee that the pair of them will have created a special dinner.'

Alastair's secretary met them in the spacious hall of the

house and was introduced as Mrs MacGregor. She was a fresh faced lady in her fifties who had the prettiness of a woman who was allowing her hair to go grey naturally so that it matched her skin tone. Without fuss, Ruth was shown to a bedroom on the first floor. It was a huge room and through the low window Ruth saw the beam of the Sanda lighthouse. The next door bathroom matched the bedroom in size with an enamelled bath in the centre of the floor.

'I'll bring one of Alastair's dressing gowns for you. Mine would be a bit short. Anything else you may need should be in the cabinet.' Mrs MacGregor pointed to a corner. 'Tell me what you would like to drink and I'll send Alastair up with it.'

By the time the bath was filled Alastair still hadn't appeared. Ruth sat for a minute or two wearing the bulky woollen dressing gown but eventually she dropped it on a chair and slipped into the foamy water. She had barely settled when there was a knock at the door and she heard the voice of her host apologising for the delay. The bath salts in the soft water had created suds which covered her except head and shoulders.

'Come in,' she called. 'The door isn't locked.'

He deposited a tall clinking glass of orange juice on the side of the bath and grinned at her. 'I suppose the next question would be – would you like me to do your back?'

Ruth laughed. 'The honest answer could well be yes. But in this lovely soft water it isn't necessary. Off you go boy and give a girl peace to enjoy luxury. Will Mrs MacGregor mind if I come down to dinner in your dressing gown? I feel deliciously lazy.'

'She's gone up to her own flat. I won't mind a bit and there's a lovely log fire' she was told.

She came downstairs to find him sitting by the fire in an oak panelled room lit only by a single lamp and the flickering flames. A table had been set for two well within the heat throwing range of the large grate. The atmosphere was lazy and luxurious.

'Are you ready to eat? Everything is either in the fridge or the oven.' He stood up. 'Would you like red or white wine?'

'Neither, if you don't mind. I've never developed a taste for alcohol. But you go ahead and I'll have another glass of orange juice.'

Again came his quick smile. 'I'll join you in the orange juice. There's no fun in entertaining a sober girl when you're drunk.'

The meal was delicious. They started with a salad of crab meat to which fruit had been added, followed by a beef fillet with baked and roast potatoes and a mixture of steamed vegetables. Next appeared a trifle with thick pouring cream.

'I'll come and do the dishes,' said Ruth when Alastair rose to make coffee but he held up his hand to stop her. 'I had strict instructions that they were just to be left in the sink. I wouldn't dare disobey.'

Afterwards they sat talking on either side of the fire. Ruth learned that Alastair and his parents had been surprised by the scale of his aunt's interests. Her father died fairly young as the delayed result of war wounds and she had survived death duties to preserve the estate as well as most of his business. Inflation had increased the capital value to an astronomical sum. 'There are still some things that I haven't quite got a grip on but both she and her father were good employers so, as a result, they had loyal staff. Without that it would have been a shambles.'

It was only two months since Alastair had made a short visit to Kenya and had seen her mother and father and also spent a night with Iain and his family. 'Your father looks well but he has aged a bit. But your mother hasn't changed in all the years that I've known her,' he said.

Ruth glanced at her watch which told her that it was near midnight. 'Time for bed. It's been a long day,' she said as she rose.

'Do you want to give the hospital a ring before you turn in?'

To her surprise the nurse who answered told her that Dr

MacKenzie was still there and she was worried until he came to the phone.

'I didn't like to leave Mary earlier but they've just taken her off to bed. John is now sleeping peacefully. Phone us again in the morning but it looks as though you can enter this one on the success side of the balance sheet.'

She relayed the news to Alastair. 'Thank you for all you've done and not least for a lovely evening.'

'Sleep well,' he said and kissed her lightly.

Her bed was warm and Alastair's pyjamas were a perfect fit. Through the open curtain she could see the sweep of the lighthouse and the flickering block which told of a cruise liner heading out towards the Atlantic.

She awoke to broad daylight and Mrs MacGregor standing by her bedside with a tray of tea.

A phone call to the hospital confirmed that young John was maintaining progress.

'Why did Shorty call you big Dunlop?' she asked Alastair as he dropped her off at her house.

'Och, it's an old joke. Dunlops have forever been Makkin Tyres.

CHAPTER 21

A chastened Colonel Paterson was first in her morning surgery. He obviously hadn't slept and Ruth found herself feeling sorry for him. 'Go to bed when you get home,' she told him. 'I'll give you something to help you to sleep. It's early days to be completely certain but unless he's very unlucky your grandson shouldn't be all that long until he is home.'

'I'll never be able to thank you enough. And if ever there is anything that I can do to help you just let me know.' This was said with no trace of his former pomposity.

'There is something. You're a man of some influence,' she began but he interrupted her.

'I thought that I was until yesterday,. Now I think that I'm just a bloody old fool.'

Ruth laughed. 'Well, you're still our local councillor so I'll plant this seed in your mind and leave you to think about it. I feel that we could justify the appointment of a surgeon at the local hospital. There are many things which could be done without the trauma to the patient of being taken to Glasgow.'

There were several more patients and Ruth was finishing with one when her phone rang. Alastair's voice was urgent. 'Ruth, one of my men has been badly hurt by a cow. It looks like another Glasgow job. I'll get the plane ready. He's at the house.'

Ruth glanced into the waiting room to see only two patients who would both be there for repeat prescriptions and a blether. Hastily she assured herself that none of them needed seeing urgently then she called Dr Marshall's number.

'If necessary can you fly to Glasgow with a patient right away?'

'Yes. Where from?' A lifetime of dealing with emergencies came across in the calm voice.

'The Estate. A farm accident. Come to the house.'

'Right, I'll be there in ten minutes.'

Ruth arrived to find the stretcher of the day before again pressed into service but the young man lying in the hall of Alastair's house needed no padding to help him fill it. The parts of his face which weren't muddied were drained of any colour and his breathing was shallow and jerky, but he showed his teeth in a faint smile when Ruth dropped to her knees beside him. He was wearing a boilersuit from which all the buttons had been torn. The shirt beneath had also suffered though the belt of his trousers had survived.

Something about the shape of his features struck a familiar chord to Ruth. 'What's your name?' she asked.

'MacDonald.' Then again came the smile. 'I'm Wee Shorty.'

Ruth glanced along his length which covered at least six feet. 'You're going to be a big lad when you grow up,' she told him. He started to laugh but stopped with a grimace of pain.

When Ruth drew his clothes to the side she saw the reason. All visible parts of his body were a mass of bruises. Even Ruth's very gentle probing was enough to make him gasp. She loosened his belt and slid her hand under his trousers but the damage seemed to be confined to his upper body.

'Can you tell me what happened?'

'Aye.' His speech was slow and laboured. 'I was injecting a calf an never thocht aboot the mother. She's usually a quiet coo. But the calf let oot a bellow an' she charged an' knocked me doon. Afore Ah could roll away she got doon on her knees on my chest. Then the boss cam' runnin' an' she took off.'

There was the sound of a car on the gravel and Shorty and Dr Marshall hurried in. The wee man was wearing trousers and a shirt with the sleeves rolled above the elbows and had obviously abandoned whatever work he had been doing.,

'Thanks for phonin',' he said to Mrs MacGregor.

'Wee Shorty told me where you were,' she explained.

'An whit huv you been daein?' as he leaned over the stretcher.

'Juist followin' ma faither.'

'Whit dae ye mean?'

'Well, Ah did somethin stupid.'

The wee man laughed but when his son attempted the same he stopped with a grimace of pain.

Came the sound of a hard driven engine and Alastair appeared. He looked at Ruth and she nodded.

'How are you going to take the stretcher to the plane?'

'Land Rover. I've just brought it up,' he told her.

'Right. You go ahead. I'll phone the hospital and scribble a note. Dr Marshall will fly with you.'

By the time Ruth reached the plane the stretcher was aboard and Shorty was making it secure. Two other grave faced farm workers were standing by the Land Rover. Ruth answered Dr Marshall's question.

'There's obviously a few broken ribs and a heavy beast like that crashing down on his chest must have done internal damage. There doesn't appear to be any injuries to the lower abdomen.'

Shorty jumped down from the door of the plane.

'Right Doc, we're ready to go,' he said to Dr Marshall before turning to Ruth. 'Could ye find a meenit tae drop in an hae a word wi' the wife?' he asked anxiously. 'She's an awfy worrier. Tell her ah'll be back before tea time.'

'Dae ye want a jaiket Shorty?' one of the other men shouted as he turned towards the plane.

'Huvvens naw,' came over his shoulder. 'Ah'm sweatin' wi' fright at the thocht o' flyin' wi' big Dunlop. Ah've seen him wi' a tractor.'

They watched the plane take off towards the sea then turn to disappear north between Sanda island and the mainland. Ruth elected to walk back to her car while the men took the Land Rover.

Mrs MacGregor came out with an offer of a coffee which was declined. They stood talking for a moment then Ruth continued the conversation through the open door of the car. Suddenly Mrs MacGregor appeared to be listening to something else then she gasped and pointed. The plane was flying low down the glen towards the landing field. Ruth was at the gate of the field as it touched down and she waited as it turned at the far end and came back towards her. It stopped, the door opened, the doctor climbed down with his back towards her then turned. The front of his clothes were saturated with blood. 'I'm sorry, Ruth, we've lost him' he said. 'There must have been massive internal bleeding. We had hardly levelled off when it happened. He vomited, apologised to us for making a mess, then collapsed.'

She was almost by the door of the plane when Shorty jumped down. 'I'm sorry, Shorty,' she said. 'Maybe I should have tried to get him to the local hospital.'

This strong wee man, five inches shorter than herself, put a hand on each of her shoulders. His face had lost colour but his voice was level and controlled. 'Listen, lass, there's naebody tae blame for this, no even Wee Shorty himsel' for he wis juist daein as we aye did. An' you did whit both you an' Dr Marshall thocht wis for the best. He brocht that boy intae the world an' if he had thocht ye were wrang he'd soon hae telt ye. These things happen, an' it's no for us tae be askin' why. It's oor job tae get on wi' whits left.'

Ruth took Shorty home. 'He wis oor only wean,' he told her. 'She hadna an easy time. She wantit tae try for a wee lassie but I wis feart. Ah didna want tae lose her. It's no easy tae ken when ye're right an noo it looks lake Ah wis wrang.'

The house was a stone built farm cottage. The approach was by a long track which from the road looked to be almost level but in fact was on a continuous rising plane. When Ruth turned the final dogleg she saw that it enjoyed a lovely view. Although still wearing its winter clothes the garden was neat and tidy and ready to welcome the spring. A heavy built woman, not far short of Ruth's own height and wearing a flowered wrap around apron emerged from the door and awaited their approach.

'Angus is gone.' Her words were more statement of fact than question.

'He's gone Flora. But he went quickly wae nae pain.' Shorty showed no surprise that she should be aware of what had happened.

'Well that's aye a bit o' comfort,' she answered her husband matter of factly and explained. 'Ah saw the plane comin' back. Ah kent then.' She turned to Ruth. 'Come away in Doctor, ye'll be ready for a cup o' tea.' While the kettle was boiling she went to a corner press and came back with a glass of whisky. Their fingers touched as she handed it to Shorty. This was the first physical contact that Ruth had seen between the bereaved parents.

Although there were tears behind her eyes the mother had complete control of her emotions. Ruth visited again in the evening but her offer of an aid to sleep was declined. In her home country, despite the stoicism of the menfolk there were few women who did not give way to emotion and over the next few days she began to worry about this mother who seemed unwilling to grieve over the death of her only child.

About a week after the funeral a young girl appeared at evening surgery. A quick glance at her card told Ruth that she was twenty years old and the pencilled notation of Dr Marshall was 'A daughter anyone would be proud of'. The girl was well dressed but her features were white and strained and her eyes showed evidence of recent crying. Just outside in the fading light a thrush was using the still evening air to project his song and his success could be clearly heard inside the room.

The girl listened for a moment. 'Lovely, isn't it?' she said then burst out, 'I'm pregnant.'

'Are you sure?'

'Oh yes. There's no doubt.'

Ruth glanced again at the card for confirmation. 'I see you aren't married. Do you know who the father is?'

'Oh yes. There's never been anyone else.' The tone was defensive then, 'I'm sorry. I forgot that you're not long here and wouldn't know. It's Angus MacDonald.' Floods of fresh tears followed.

Ruth went to the door to check that there were no other patients then came back to sit down. 'Now,' she said 'we'll attend to the practicalities before we start to worry about anything else.'

As the doctor made her examination, took blood pressure and worked out dates, the girl told her story.

The young couple had courted from schooldays but, partly through fear of pregnancy, had avoided sex. Then, late in a particularly warm evening the previous summer they had been walking on the beach. The sand was hot and the water looked cool. They had gone for a swim and the dam of behaviour was breached. This became a regular occurrence and they became increasingly careless with predictable results.

After a few weeks of worry they had finally plucked up the courage to tell her parents on the night before Wee Shorty's death. 'We were so nervous and didn't quite know what they would say.' She smiled before going on. 'Angus said that it was his fault and so he should be the one to confess. He finally got round to it in the middle of supper. Dad laughed, Mum blushed. Then they told us that a score of years back they themselves had been in an exactly similar situation.'

'We were going to tell Angus' parents the following night. But now I just don't know how I can do it. His mother was such fun but now she seems to have built a shell round herself and even his poor wee father is being shut out. Dad and Mum offered to go with me but that seems too much like a scene from a bad film.'

Ruth thought for a moment. 'Do your parents know that you were coming here to see me tonight?' she asked.

'Oh yes.'

'Well, I had been meaning to drop up to see the Mac-Donalds anyway. Would you like to come with me? You could decide how you want to play it once we see how they are.'

'Could I? They think the world of you.' Her face brightened.

'Maybe you should give your parents a ring and see what they think of the idea. If they approve I could go now.'

Although it was almost dark Shorty was puttering in the garden when they drove up. If he was surprised to see them together he didn't show it but his pleasure wasn't concealed. 'Come awa' in. The wife's by the fire,' and he ushered them ahead of him. Flora MacDonald was knitting but laid down her needles and wool and stood up. Silently she looked at the young girl then at the doctor before her gaze returned to the girl. Then, softly she spoke.

'Kirsty, huv you come tae tell what I think ye've come tae tell?' Kirsty nodded silently. With four short running steps she had reached the girl to enfold her in a bear hug. Then enormous sobs began to wrench her body.

Her husband touched Ruth on the arm and nodded towards the door. 'We'll just leave them be for a whiley,' he said softly.

It wasn't until she was outside that Ruth realised that Flora MacDonald had been knitting a white baby jacket.

'Aboot a month ago Flora said she thought that there wis somethin' in the wind,' Shorty explained. 'We were juist waitin' tae let the young yins tell us in their ain time. Then when naething was said we were feart that we have been wrang. It's no gaun tae be easy for Kirsty noo but we'll help all we can an' her parents are gran' folk. We juist thocht that we had been so lucky.'

Ruth had never given more than a passing glance towards psychology but instead of settling to sleep she sat up in bed looking through the open curtains to the sparkle of the moon on the ripple of the tide and thinking of how different were the reactions of people to roughly comparable situations.

Margaret Thompson had reacted with anger against her dead husband and resentment of her innocent daughter. Yet this had been vanquished by nothing more than a friendly wee terrier dog. Mary Paterson accepted the fact that she had lost her husband and her son had lost his father simply through the carelessness of somebody else. And she accepted her arrogant father-in-law as part of her duty and role in life. Flora MacDonald had been devastated until she had confirmation that her son lived on in the womb of his girlfriend. She thought of Alastair telling her how her father had aged and wondered what her own thoughts would be when, if events followed their natural course, he was dead and she still alive. She had always accepted her mother as mortal but even as an experienced doctor she still tended to think of her father as being indestructible.

She fell asleep on thoughts of Lachie and Kate who had lived and died together and hoped that they would have considered herself and her brother a credit to their love and care.

Still in a sitting position she was wakened in broad daylight by the telephone. The parade ground voice of Colonel Paterson informed that his daughter-in-law and grandson were coming home on the morning plane.

'I'd appreciate it if you could call in sometime this afternoon just to check over the wee chap. The hospital say that he is all right but I'd like you to be satisfied before taking him out.'

Ruth replaced the bedside receiver with the thought that she had probably been paid the highest compliment that it was in the power of the colonel to bestow. That afternoon she was met at the door by a very fit looking wee boy. He and his grandfather set off for a walk and the doctor and his mother sat down with mugs of tea. Mary Paterson was bright and animated.

'You look as though you had been on holiday,' Ruth told her.

Mary was serious for a moment then, 'You know to a certain extent I have been. I'd no idea how wearing life with grandpa was until I escaped for a while. Once I knew that John was going to get better I could relax.' Then with a slight but noticeable blush, 'George MacKenzie took me out a few times. It was just so nice to have male conversation with someone nearer my own age.'

During the next half hour Ruth brought her up to date with some of the happenings while she had been away. Mary cried when she was told of the death of Wee Shorty. 'He was just a bigger version of his father and with the same good nature. I'd like to go to see Flora. Do you think I should?'

'Yes I do and take John with you. Flora will be all right but she needs company.'

The return of the Paterson men brought a bustle of movement. Ruth rose to leave but was stopped by the colonel. He had followed up her suggestion of the appointment of a surgeon and found that the idea carried a lot of support. One councillor who was an accountant was working on figures which he was sure were going to prove that there could be a substantial saving of money over the cost of sending patients to Glasgow by air ambulance.

Ruth was restless in the evening. She stood for a time in her garden then decided to drive round to visit Marie Sinclair. She arrived to find an empty house. She stood looking out to sea then her eye was caught by the light of Margaret Thompson's house on the opposite side of the glen.

Margaret was reading a newspaper by the fire but there was the gentle rumble of a man's voice from the bedroom. 'James is reading a story to Jennifer but he should soon be joining us. I always know when Jennifer is falling asleep. His voice gets softer and softer.' She rose to put on a kettle.

Her prediction proved correct and James came through as the kettle boiled. After some general conversation he turned to Margaret. 'Did you tell Dr MacLeod?' he asked.

'No, I didn't, but she's going to find it strange if my daughter addresses her as Auntie Ruth and my husband addresses her so formally.'

Ruth gave a cry of delight. 'When is this going to happen?' she asked.

It was James who answered. 'Not until the autumn. My

mother-in-law is talking of selling her house and moving nearer the village and we think that would be best for her. But if we were to get married now and she had the clear nights of the summer to get used to living on her own she might just decide to wait where she is. Long term this wouldn't be good for her.'

CHAPTER 22

Easter brought holidaymakers and an increase of work for Ruth. Twice within a week she had to call out the air ambulance. One of these calls was in the middle of a stormy night to pick up a nine year old boy whose inflamed appendix had perforated before the child reached hospital. On the second occasion the aircraft had just left with a patient from the town practice and had to make another trip by return.

At the end of a morning surgery she checked her waiting room to find a tall well built man sitting reading a magazine. He rose to his feet and held out his hand. 'Hullo Ruth,' he said with an easy smile. It took a few seconds to recognise George MacKenzie whom she hadn't seen since college days.

'I came down last night and I'm staying with the Patersons,' he explained. 'The old boy's a bit formidable though' he added.

Since graduation he had spent all his time working in city hospitals. The long hours had given him both wealth and a breadth of experience but on a couple of occasions had driven him close to breakdown. Mary Paterson had told him of the move to appoint a general surgeon at the local hospital and he was giving serious thought to applying for the post if it was created.

Ruth wondered how much of this was due to a wish to be nearer Mary but she also remembered him as a conscientious and able student and hoped that his interest would continue. It had been he who had operated on the child in the early morning hours so he had obviously been keeping up with his surgery. His friendship with Mary Paterson could only be good for her and her young son.

Once things had quietened down, Ruth found that she had time for an afternoon walk. As she set off the day was dull so rather than take to the fields she decided to follow the road towards the shore. There was a car parked in a lay-by but she paid it scant attention as she stood to watch a pair of oyster catchers pair bonding on the beach. A couple of hundred yards further on a protrusion of rock pointed to the Antrim coast. A woman and child stood on this and when they moved Ruth saw that it was Mary Paterson and John.

The sun broke the clouds as Ruth climbed the bank from the road and as she neared the pair she could see a trail of bubbles far out in the water. Then a black, seal like object broke the surface and an arm waved. John waved back vigorously then began to investigate the rock pools which had been left by the falling tide. His mother's cheeks had been fanned to a glow by the light wind.

'That's George,' she explained. 'He had his skin diving kit in the boot of his car.'

'He's gone to catch clams for our tea,' her son put in before resuming his own quest.

'Why don't you come round for your tea?' said his mother. Then, when Ruth hesitated, 'Don't worry if he doesn't catch anything. I've got plenty other things in reserve. And Granda is at a meeting this afternoon so he will have the latest news on the appointment of a surgeon.'

Ruth agreed to be there or to let her know if she had a call out then resumed her walk. She stood for a time listening to the noisily mating fulmars on the cliffs which had caused the air pocket when young John was being taken to hospital. Then she dropped to the shore and began to walk the long beach toward the dark mass of the Mull of Kintyre.

One of her patients was an elderly bachelor farmer. He lived on his own in rather rough conditions but Ruth never left his company without the feeling that she had been privy to communion with the best brain that ever she had met. He was a lonely, rather solitary man. He had a wide forehead and heavy beetle eyebrows which sheltered the misty blue eyes of a deep thinker. He was a voracious reader and, appreciative of an intelligent ear, taught the young doctor much about the ancient history of the area.

She watched the damp sand change colour with each step as her weight forced out the water and thought of the other feet which had trod the same sand over the centuries. Here the ancient peoples from the shores of the Mediterranean had probably rested three and a half thousand years ago before continuing their journey north to become the first people of Orkney.

Here Columba and his followers had pulled their coracle ashore so that they could build a fire and sleep in the dry luxury of the Pipers Cave in the cliffs before tackling the vicious tides to round the Mull and touch Islay, before going on to Iona. Here, centuries later, the Norsemen had rested after surviving these same tides only to go on to a disastrous defeat at the Battle of Largs.

Within the span of Ruth's own lifetime German submarines had surfaced to charge their batteries under the cover of darkness before resuming their pillage of the merchant ships entering the North Channel from the Atlantic. Thoughts of war cast her mind back to the troubles which had torn her own country and how her father had kept control of his district with an iron hand in a velvet glove.

Some way in front she could see a young family of a mother and two children building sand castles. As she neared them a little terrier dog ran towards her, whirled in the sand immediately in front of her feet and rolled over on his back in a position where she just had to tickle his tummy. Then the children shouted. He scrambled to his feet and ran towards them. When he was close they jumped back from their construction and then screamed with delight as their pet turned on his back and wriggled until he had demolished their efforts. Ruth stopped to speak to the mother then walked on escorted by the dog until another cry from the children brought him back to duty.

Not for the first time she felt a pang of envy. Then she thought of Margaret Thompson and Mary Paterson. Perhaps this also was a young mother whose mask of joy hid a face of sadness.

Her reverie was interrupted by a shout and she looked up to see a horseman cantering towards her on the firm sand by the water's edge. As he got nearer she recognised the broad shoulders of Alastair MacIntyre and as he drew his mount to a prancing walk she thought that the muscular animal resembled its owner in appearance and seemed to have the same zest for life. However, when brought to a halt, pressure on the reins was sufficient to keep it standing perfectly still.

'I'd been meaning to come to see you tomorrow,' said Alastair without dismounting. 'Can you come on the length of the house just now? We could have a blether, then you could share my dinner and I'll leave you home.'

'Alastair I'd love to but I can't stay to dinner. Somebody else is going to feed me tonight,' and she explained.

'Well, come for a cup of coffee just now if only to reassure Mrs MacGregor that we're still speaking to one another,' he pleaded. 'She keeps asking about you.'

Ruth laughed then glanced over her shoulder at the intervening river as she agreed. Alastair knotted the reins, laid them in front of the saddle, then slid backwards, still keeping his feet in the stirrups.

'Stand,' he commanded firmly then told Ruth to stand with her back to the horse and reach up her arms. He leant down, grasped her wrists and with a quick grunt of effort lifted her so that one leg swung over the neck of the horse and she landed in the saddle in front of him. The horse never moved a muscle although her right foot had passed close to his eye. But Ruth was indignant.

'You big fool,' she scolded. 'I weigh over 150 pounds and you shouldn't lift anything near that weight while putting all the strain on your back muscles.'

'Yes doctor,' he laughed and as he reached round for the reins he gave her a quick cuddle. 'Now,' he continued, 'if I hear any more lectures I'll dump you in the river as we cross.'

Mrs MacGregor was obviously pleased to see her and sat

talking while Alastair attended to his horse. Then she left them alone with a tray of coffee and freshly made pancakes and Ruth learned why Alastair had been planning to visit her. He carried an accident insurance policy on behalf of his staff. He had written to the company after the death of Wee Shorty. They were accepting liability but wanted a copy of the death certificate.

He smiled. 'I went to see the MacDonalds. They told me about the baby. They want this money, and it will be a considerable sum, to be paid into a trust fund which Kirsty can use as and when she needs it. They would like you and me to be trustees of that fund. They want us to take wide enough powers to deal with anything that might come up. Are you willing to take it on?'

'When I came here I wasn't sure how people would react to having a young black female doctor. Now something like this helps me to answer the doubt. Yes, of course I'll take it on.'

As Alastair was leaving her home he asked about George MacKenzie.

'You quite fancied Mary, didn't you?' Ruth teased.

'She's a bonny girl. And oh boy, what legs. But it will take a braver man than me to take on the colonel as a surrogate father-in-law. Do you think this man will get the surgeon's job?'

'It's not yet certain that the appointment will come off, but if it does I'd like to see him there.'

If Ruth had lacked first hand knowledge of the pompous Colonel Paterson she would not have recognised him as the same man who, that evening, was to entertain her as host. The colonel and George MacKenzie were settled on either side of a glowing coal fire while his daughter-in-law worked in the kitchen. Young John was perched on his grandfather's knee and each man had a golden glass at his elbow. At the table the conversation was interesting and wide ranging with nobody holding monopoly.

About a fortnight later Ruth had an evening phone call

from Alastair. 'When can you take time off to rejuvenate a tired old farmer?'

She laughed. 'With so many fit young farmers around it seems like a waste of time to bother rejuvenating a tired old one.'

They agreed to try and spend the following Saturday together if Ruth's morning surgery turned up no problems. The weather decided to be kind and Ruth had the sun on her head as she put walking boots into the well of the back seats of her car. As she drove round, every field by the roadside had replete lambs taking advantage of the heat and she arrived to find Alastair and Mrs MacGregor sitting out with mugs of coffee. The normally rather severe secretary was dressed in shorts and a light top.

It was Alastair who went inside to bring out another mug. 'He's still brooding over the death of Wee Shorty,' Ruth was told anxiously. 'I've made up a picnic for you in a haversack.'

When coffee was disposed of Ruth changed her footwear while Alastair went off to reappear carrying a haversack and two walking sticks. 'If we follow the burn we'll meet the new Glen road and that will give easier walking until near the top of the cliffs. Then we can keep in sight of the sea for a couple of miles or so. We can cross the lighthouse road at the Gap. But if you get tired we can follow the road to here.' He smiled. 'Do you think you're fit for a ten mile round?'

'Don't worry, son, Mummy will give you a piggy back over the rougher bits,' she told him.

They followed the chuckling burn for almost an hour before crossing to climb the hill to the road. As they neared the Glen house the wife of the shepherd came out to meet them. 'Could I tempt you to a cup of tea or a cold drink?' she asked.

From there it was a steady climb and the heat began to take its toll. Although both of them had grown up in a land of much higher temperature, even Ruth was bathed in sweat by the time they breasted the top to look down to the Smugglers Cut where the remains of the Boy Robert could just be seen beneath the low tide. The atmosphere was particularly clear and it was almost possible to believe the legend of the giant stepping from Ireland to Rathlin and then to the Mull of Kintyre where they stood. A golden eagle flew off the cliff to their left and they could clearly see its mate sitting on a nest. The grazing sheep paid no attention but the nesting fulmars on the next face nearer the shore set up a raucous cry of defence.

'Do the eagles take lambs?' asked Ruth.

'This nest has been occupied for a number of years and so far as we know we haven't lost any lambs to it. But the shepherds tell me that they have lost lambs to eagles on other hills where they have worked.'

The bird in flight was hovering on almost motionless wings just below their level not more than a hundred yards away. Suddenly it powered to the ground, there was a short sharp squeal of fright and it rose to the nest with a mountain hare in its talons.

'It seems a pity for something to die on such a lovely day but at least it died quickly' said Ruth.

'The eagle only killed because it was hungry,' she was told. 'Man is one of the very few species which kill for reasons other than necessity. And talking of such things, do you want to picnic here or farther on our way?'

'So long as you don't mind carrying the load I'd rather wait. If I eat now I'll get lazy and want to take the shortest way home.'

They walked south west holding the ridge as much as possible so that they had a view both to left and right. To the left they could see over Sanda island to Ailsa Craig and the Ayrshire coast. To the right the broad Atlantic leapt Rathlin to roll unhindered all the way to America. In front, tractors could be seen working in the fields of Antrim before they dipped into the glen to climb the other side above Ballymontgomery. When they gained the Height of Eagle Rock they turned to look backwards.

Round the shoulder of the hill they had just left the Rhinns of Islay pointed towards Colonsay. The dark volcanic peaks of the Paps of Jura seemed to poke holes in the blue of the sky. As they resumed their journey Alastair, who was leading, stopped and help up his hand. Ruth looked round his shoulder. About ten yards in front a pair of twin roe deer calves were regarding them curiously through four amber eyes. Apart from twitching their ears they showed no concern at the sight of what would almost certainly be their first human beings. They lay beneath the slight overhang of a sun warmed rock and couldn't have been more than a day old.

'It's early in the year to see calves,' said Alastair when they have given the rock a wide berth. 'But so long as the mother can keep them out of sight of the eagle for a few days they should survive.'

They dipped to the road, climbed the bank on the other side, walked for another five minutes and then Alastair jumped into a small grassy hollow, turned and bowed. 'Would madam care to enter the dining room?' he smiled.

The grass of the hollow was dry and warm. From a sitting position they had a panorama of azure sea titillating the Irish coast from Ballycastle to Larne but simply by lying back they would be invisible from not more than a few yards. From the haversack Alastair produced a small tablecloth which he laid between them. On this was placed the plastic containers which, when opened, disclosed contents of chicken legs, cold sausages and buttered bread. The square was completed by a fourth which housed a bunch of grapes and a pack of cheese which had been diced. Two bakelite plates, cups of the same material and a flask of tea exhausted the cornucopia. He opened the bag and shook it, then laughed 'She's forgotten the forks.' But fingers proved to be perfectly adequate. Between each course Alastair brought bunches of cool, damp sphagnum moss to wash their hands. Ruth didn't want to tell him that she would have quite liked to allow the taste to linger on her fingers.

When they had eaten Alastair repacked the haversack with the debris then lay back on the short springy grass with the bag beneath his head. It seemed natural for Ruth to use his stomach as her pillow. A lark rose some distance away and drifted in the slight breeze until it had taken its song directly overhead. A bumble bee swooped over the edge of their refuge but finding the haven occupied flew off transmitting a noisy protest. A small clump of hardy primroses were left for investigation at a later date.

Ruth closed her eyes and allowed the glow of the sun to submerge her to that comfortable state where her body was lethargic and her mind active. As the wings of memory carried her back for more than thirty years she thought of the mix of circumstances which had brought her, a black girl from a bush hut in central Africa, to picnic with a wealthy laird on the far west coast of Scotland. She thought of her father, orphaned at an early age, then being brought up surrounded by a level of love and care far greater than ever would have been provided by his natural parents. She thought of how his adoptive parents had instilled in him a faith in God and a belief and pride in himself which, in turn, he had passed on to his children.

Her first meeting with Lachie and Kate MacKinnon was in the lazy reaches of her memory but even now, so long after their death, their features and lilting voices were crystal clear. She remembered the fun Lachie took from talking to her in Gaelic and then correcting her mispronunciation of words. She remembered her father and Roddy MacLean, two hugely powerful men, their faces streaked by tears, coming to tell her that never again would she be cuddled in either pair of these comfortable chubby arms.

She remembered coming to London and how James Wright had saved her faith in human nature. So many folk had then, in a fairly short time, had an influence in her life, The Wrights, their daughter Helen and their son-in-law Tommy Fraser, the Murrays and their later to be son-in-law Bob Hamilton, Jock MacRae and his fast and compassionate dispatch of the wounded deer hind and her calf, and big John MacKinnon with his love for Kate's mother had all, in their various ways, played their part.

She recalled her father taking her to meet Davie and Elaine Sinclair, then how Elaine and her mother Katherine had equally accepted that, despite a stillborn daughter and grand-daughter, they were greatly blessed to have a live son and grandson. She thought of Davie's mother Marie, this serene woman who had become her closest confidante. Then a Puck-like face topped by a shock of black hair flecked with grey filled the vision of her memory. Tears forced themselves through her closed eyelids and a massive sob heaved her body. This sheltered hollow at the point of the Mull of Kintyre became the open top of Cnocan Lin.

Jock Spence, that massive wee giant of a man, seemed to be smiling down at her. She had loved him, but she had loved him as the second father which he had become. As the thought crystallised she realised that she loved this man whose flank was cradling her head. But this was a loin stirring love of a type which she had never previously known. Alastair moved her head to his thigh and sat up. She opened her eyes to look into the blue eyes which twinkled back. Slowly he bent to kiss her long and deeply. This no longer was the man who for so long she had regarded as a brother.

The miles home seemed but yards. As, hand in hand, they walked up the curved gravel drive, the door opened. Mrs MacGregor watched them coming closer, then ran to clasp Ruth in a massive hug. She turned, shook hands formally with Alastair, then threw her arms round his neck. 'I couldn't be more happy,' said this normally undemonstrative woman before turning to run back into the house. No other words had been spoken.

The young couple looked at one another and laughed. 'Psychic' said Alastair. 'Or maybe she had put something in the tea,' he added dryly.

CHAPTER 23

Ruth delivered Kirsty's baby on a dry September morning which Kirsty's father described as 'drouthy'. The baby was born at home. On the previous evening Ruth had called to find Kirsty, her mother and Flora MacDonald calmly chattering over a cheerful fire.

'Go you to bed Doctor. We'll phone when we need you.'

'Where are the menfolk?' asked Ruth.

'Och we sent them to the pub,' it was Kirsty's mother who answered. 'Honestly, how these craturs manage to calve cows and lamb ewes I'll never know. The way they were acting you would think that birthing a baby was an international undertaking.'

Ruth's phone rang just after five in the morning.

'Fairly soon now Doctor,' came the calm voice of Mrs Black. 'She's been working for the past half hour.'

'Balach beag,' said Ruth when she wrapped the baby in a towel.

'Taing do Dhia,' said Flora MacDonald.

'Good morning, Angus Black MacDonald,' said Kirsty when the bundle was laid at her breast.

Ruth was putting thought towards her own wedding. She had written to Iain for his advice on bringing her parents. His view was that they would want to come but the cold of a Scottish winter could be too much of a change for them. It was decided that they should travel to Scotland around the middle of August and that the wedding would be in the second week of September.

'If the big fella works hard enough we should be far enough on wi' the hervest tae let him huv a day or two off bae then,' Shorty informed her.

Serene and elderly, Samuel and Naomi descended to the

adopted land of their daughter at Glasgow airport. The day was dry with just a hint of heat haze. Alastair and Ruth met them with his own light plane. Knowing the phlegmatic character of her father Ruth has been confident that the journey would cause him little concern, but she had worried about her mother. Neither of them had flown before.

However, when Alastair levelled off to his cruising height above the Firth of Clyde she realised that her fears had been needless. Not only did Naomi show no sign of tiredness but she looked to be thoroughly enjoying herself. They flew low over the heel of the hand of Kintyre to see Ruth's house and the beach of Dunaverty from the air then swung out to sea to approach the landing strip over the course of the river. This gave the best view of the 'Big Hoose' as it faced the sea to the south but also profiled the hump of Cnocan Lin to the north.

Mrs MacGregor met them as they landed and slightly disconcerted the undemonstrative Samuel by giving him a cuddle. She and Naomi met in a massive hug.

Despite their interest in the large house that was soon to be home to their daughter, the length of their journey was shown in the bearing of the old couple by the time that they had finished a cup of tea. Ruth took them off to her own house. When they had settled for the night and she was reflecting on the events of the day Ruth realised that for the first time in her life her mother had gone upstairs to bed.

Next morning she emerged from her own room to the landing to find her father, mug of tea in hand, sitting on the top step of her stair and studying the mural of Cnocan Lin.

'Couldn't you sleep, Dad?' she asked anxiously.

'Indeed I slept well. Your mother is still asleep,. But it is some hours since my body clock told me that it was sun up. Tell me, is that a painting of the Boundary Hill?'

Ruth laughed. 'There are so few Gaelic speakers left here that I have never heard it called that. But, yes, that is Cnocan Lin where Jock used to take me for a walk. Would you like to go up there?'

'Indeed I would. When I see you here I realise how much I owe to the memory of Iain Beag.'

Naomi elected to sit in the sun with Marie outside her house while father and daughter made the gentle climb. Both going up and down they drank cool, clear water from the jar which Jock had left at the spring years before. At the top they stood in a sacred silence dedicated to the memory of the short-legged giant who had done so much to bring them together to this place.

The sun warmed their backs and cast their shadows into the hanging valley immediately beneath them. In the main valley tractor drawn trailers were trundling towards their parent farms bearing loads of oat sheaves which would ensure survival of stock during the coming winter. A large white cruise liner, the sun winking on the glass of its portholes, seemed to sail out of the cliffs of the Mull to cleave a furrow in the smooth blue of the sea. As they turned to leave, a covey of grouse, which had escaped the onslaught of the Twelfth, rose and go-backed their way along the ridge.

During the weeks before the wedding, Samuel and Naomi quietly worked at familiarising themselves as far as possible with this area where Ruth had chosen to live. One day Ruth arrived home to find Naomi making the lunch with no sign of her father whom she found sitting on the roadside bank at the end of the village. A clutch of wide eyed local children sat listening as the first black man that ever they had seen told them a story. At church on Sunday their velvet brown baritone and rich contralto voices greatly enhanced the quality of the singing.

Alastair and Ruth became man and wife in the local church. The reception, organised by Mrs MacGregor and the estate workers, was held in a marquee in the grounds.

'Tell them no' tae spoil the grass,' said Shorty. 'We need it for twinnin yowes in the spring.'

Alastair's parents came as did Iain, Anna and their family. Sarah, now late teenage with long brown legs barely disap-pearing into a white mini skirt brought blood pressure to bubbling point among the young lads of the district and stirred memories in the many who wished that they could again be young.

But it was her grandmother who stole the show when she walked into the small, homely church on the arm of her son. Naomi was not as tall as her daughter but, although physically as well as mentally a very strong woman, she carried little excess weight and had the same regal carriage and straight legged, swung from the hips walk. The sun shining through the stained glass windows reflected the serenity of her ebony features as she slowly made her way to the front seat. Her outfit had been made entirely by herself and owed nothing to the expensive skills of any couturier. The material was cotton and the bright autumn colour was just near enough gold to enhance her burnished skin. The design was in one piece and to the waist was moulded to her full busted body before falling to a long straight skirt which was split on one side to just above the knee. The effect was striking and elegant. A tall turban style hat in the same material completed the picture.

'My Goad,' whispered Shorty to Flora 'if the dochter looks lake that gin she's that age the big fella has fallen on his feet.'

Roddy and Fiona MacLean had travelled from their retirement home in Skye. The Wrights had come from London to stay with Helen and Tommy Fraser. The Murrays flew to Inverness then travelled down with Bob and Jackie. Mr Wright had recently retired and indulged the longing of a lifetime to buy a white Mercedes. He insisted that this had to be the bridal car. Elaine was matron of honour with Jennifer Thompson taking very seriously the duties of flower girl. Simon Itombi travelled from Nairobi to be best man. As a wedding present he brought one of his own paintings of a Kenya sunrise which made Ruth feel really homesick. The bridal party emerged from Ruth's house to find the tall handsome figure of James Wright standing beside the open door of his shining, ribbon-bedecked car with a chauffeur's hat tucked beneath his arm.

Samuel escorted Ruth down the aisle then continued his father of the bride duties with a speech at the reception. He finished to laughter by advising Alastair to chain his wife to the bed each night as she had started running away from home at the age of four.

The young couple spent a quiet week in the north of Scotland, partly to allow Ruth's parents a chance to be home and settled before flying out to spend the rest of their honeymoon with them

After much persuasion Iain had succeeded in moving them to a modern bungalow similar and close to his own. Sarah was hoping to take a degree in botany and spent much of her spare time with her grandfather in either of the two gardens. Like many of the young in a similar situation she was amazed by the breadth of knowledge possessed by the old man.

As it does with so many women who have never asked too much of life, age was treating Naomi with extreme kindness. As a young woman she had been lean. Now she enjoyed a comfortable padding but her back was straight and her hands as steady as Ruth had ever remembered them to be. As a boy Alastair had spent some of his school holidays on the farm with Roddy and Fiona MacLean's two sons. Some of his happiest memories were of spending time with this strong black man who now was his father-in-law.

Two mornings before they were due to start for home Ruth awoke to find her husband already awake and staring at the ceiling. When she tickled his chin she was surprised to find a serious face turned towards her.

'Is something wrong?' she asked anxiously.

'Not really. But I was wondering about your parents. Iain and Anna have bought them this house. I know that your father never took money for many of the things which he did for other people. I feel that we should be making some contribution but I don't quite know how to go about it. I don't want to embarrass them.'

Ruth propped herself on one elbow then leaned over to kiss him. 'You're a lovely man,' she told him. 'Talk to Iain.

I think you'll find that there isn't a problem but it will set your mind at rest. But for the next quarter of an hour you're going to talk to nobody but me.' And she kissed him again.

Iain upheld both her sentiment and her reasoning. 'Believe me, I greatly appreciate your offer but it would be wrong of me to take you up on it. When Ruth went off to Britain I was left this house, half of the value of which was hers. She wouldn't take any money. Things have gone well with me and I was able to buy the other house for our parents. When they are finished with it, it is there either to sell or as a home for one of our children if they need it.'

He gave a short laugh. 'I'm just so pleased that you and Ruth finally got married. Anna and I always thought that it would happen but by the time you got engaged we were beginning to despair.'

They left Kenya pleased that they had gone and with the promise to return before too long.

'Do not be worrying about us,' Samuel told them. 'We are comfortable and blessed to have Iain and Anna so close to us.'

But a real worry awaited them. They called on Marie on their way home and she met them solemn faced. 'What's wrong, has something happened to one of the children?' asked Ruth.

Marie turned to Alastair. 'There's a man been staying in the hotel for the past week. He claims that he is your aunt's son and that he should have inherited the estate.'

'But that's not possible. My aunt was never married.'

Ruth thought for a moment before she voiced an opinion. 'Alastair, we'll have to look into this. The fact that your aunt never married doesn't preclude her from having a son. I just feel that it's strange he never presented himself before this.'

Mrs MacGregor met them with tears in her eyes. 'Have you heard?' she asked.

'Yes,' answered Alastair. 'Has he been here?'

'Oh yes. He's been twice. What are we going to do?'

'Well, I'll have to meet him. But if he is my aunt's son we

can't deny him his right.'

After a night of little sleep Alastair phoned the legal practice which for several generations had handled the affairs of the estate. It was a long established firm which had been handed down on a father to son basis and the senior partner was now a man not much older than Alastair. His father had drawn up the will by which Alastair had inherited from his aunt and, along with the current incumbent of the post of manager at the bank, had been joint executor.

'My father was still active when your aunt's will was probated so I don't know a great deal about it. But if this man's claims are true it could have serious repercussions for our firm. Can I dig out the file and come down to see you this afternoon?'

'Your aunt's will is quite straightforward but other than that this is an interesting package,' he said that afternoon as he untied the ribbon which bound the file. 'For instance, did you know that your aunt had been born out of wedlock?'

'No. I didn't,' Alastair confessed. 'I knew that she had been about a dozen years older than my mother. Are you telling me that they weren't full sisters?'

'Oh no. It seems that your grandparents had been anticipating future events when your grandfather's regiment was suddenly posted to India. Your aunt was ten years old before they were able to marry. Under the terms of your grandfather's final will this estate was simply divided in equal value between your aunt and your mother.'

He took a sip of coffee before going on. 'This will superseded a previous will and was made just two years before his death. My father, being the cautious man that he was, preserved an unsigned copy of the original will in the file. In this will a considerable sum of money was made available to be administered at the discretion of Mr Angus MacDonald of Balachraich Cottage.'

'But that was Shorty's father,' Alastair burst out then thought for a moment before going on. 'You know this whole thing just gets more strange. Whenever I am away Shorty runs the farm side of things. He's very conscientious and will hardly leave the place. But this time there was a note left with Mrs MacGregor to say that he had unexpectedly had to go away the day before we were due to come back. I had a look around this morning and everything seems fine. I never gave it a thought until now but this makes me wonder if there's a connection.'

He rose, walked to the window and stood drinking in the view before turning back to the lawyer. 'I have loved this place since first I saw it as a wee boy. I would hate to leave it but if this man really is my aunt's son my conscience wouldn't allow me to deny his inheritance.'

'Well, as your lawyer I would advise extreme caution. If you are in any doubt at all he should be asked to prove his claim in court.'

That evening Alastair phoned the hotel and invited the man to come round for a discussion the following afternoon. Ruth was going to take her first morning surgery after their honeymoon but promised to try to be back before the meeting.

Dr Marshall had obviously done a good job in her absence and she had few patients. She was just tidying up the last of the paperwork when she saw Kirsty Black stop for a moment with her parents' car. To Ruth's surprise the passenger who alighted was Dooble Erchie. She moved to the surgery door when she heard him come into the waiting room. He was dressed in a dark suit with collar and tie. His boots shone and he obviously had taken special care with his appearance.

'Come in Archie,' she invited.

'Och well do you not think that I should be waiting a wee while. Somebody else might come,' and he moved to sit down.

'Archie, there's nobody else going to come. And anyway it wouldn't matter. Just you come away in now that you're here,' and she turned from the door leaving him no choice but to follow.

He came in and sat uncomfortably in the patients' chair.

He smoothed his hand over his white hair and then twisted his cap round and round before finally folding it into his jacket pocket.

'Now, Archie, tell me what's troubling you,' Ruth said quietly.

He looked out of the window and relief flooded his face. 'Ah here's Shorty coming now,' he beamed.

When Alastair met his guest at the door there was still no sign of his wife. The engine of the man's car was noisy but the body work was highly polished. The man himself was expensively dressed but the time he had spent in the trim of his small moustache somehow drew attention to the sallowness of his complexion and the weakness of his chin. He introduced himself as Duncan MacDonald. Alastair didn't see Ruth's car arriving but to his relief she suddenly walked into the room. He noted with some surprise that his companion did not take to his feet but merely stretched out an indifferent hand when she was introduced.

Then he launched into his story. He had been born in an Edinburgh nursing home during the 14-18 war. His mother wasn't married and he had been left for adoption. His adoptive parents had been a couple called MacDonald who had a croft in Skye. He had spent part of the 39-45 war fighting the Japanese in the Far East and after he had been demobbed he had gone back to Malaya to work on a tea plantation.

He had been home early in the fifties. At that time his parents were still quite well and he had bought them a small house for their retirement, but he wasn't long back in Malaya when his father had died. He had sent money to cover the funeral expenses and began making regular contributions towards his mother's welfare. She had died a couple of years later. Because of the distance he hadn't come home but had left the small estate to be settled up by a local lawyer. The money, which wasn't much, had gone to some obscure nephew. He had arrived back in Scotland three months ago.

His intention had been to buy a house for his eventual retirement but because he didn't quite know where he wanted to settle down he had decided to trace his real mother. This he did partly in case she might still be alive and in need of help. And, if not, he felt that to purchase a house near her home area would give him a sense of belonging which he had never really found in Skye. At this point Ruth rose and walked to the window. She twitched the curtain before lifting the sash about a couple of inches. The man's gaze followed her and he glanced out to the autumn colours of the garden.

'I had expected to find a little old lady barely getting by on a pension. You could have knocked me down with a feather when I discovered this.'

Alastair thought for a moment then asked, 'What do you propose we should do?'

'Well, as I see it you are sitting in my chair.'

'Can you prove that you are who you say that you are?'

'Come now, we're cousins and also gentlemen. Proof shouldn't be necessary.' Here he reached into the inside pocket of his jacket and brought out an envelope. 'But if you insist,' he ended as he handed this to Alastair.

The envelope contained a typed copy of a birth certificate. Alastair read it before passing it to Ruth. It gave the sex of the child as male and listed the time, date and place of birth and the name of the mother. The father of the child was given as 'Unknown soldier'.

'Oh yes,' said the man indifferently when this was pointed out, 'probably some opportunist who scented money and my poor mother was too ashamed at letting herself be used to disclose his name.'

As he was speaking Mrs MacGregor opened the door of the room. Unannounced, in walked a shining Dooble Erchie followed by a tired looking but surprisingly tidy Shorty before the door was softly closed at their back. Ruth still had the birth certificate in her hand,. 'What do you think of this?' she asked as she handed the document to Shorty.

'Och now and isn't that nice Doctor. These new fangled printing machines make a tidy job.' He handed the paper back to Ruth and reaching into his own pocket he brought out a white paper which was showing some yellow at the folds. 'But it's not at all a work of art, like this. Here, we'll let the Laird read it first,' and he passed it to the surprised Alastair who had stood up from his chair.

He found himself looking at a birth certificate written in beautiful copperplate writing. It recorded the birth of a male child in Edinburgh on the seventeenth of March 1916. The mother was listed as Caroline Jane Todd, Gentlewoman. The father was Angus John MacDonald, Shepherd. On the bottom margin was an annotation by a Church of Scotland minister to certify that Duncan Todd MacDonald had been baptised on Skye on the eighth day of June 1916.

'Shorty, where on earth did you get this?'

'Och, that's a bit o' family history that cam' oot o' the old folks kist. But Ah had tae go tae Edinburgh tae get this,' and he handed over another sheet of paper.

'But this is a death certificate,' and Alastair turned towards the man in the chair who sprang to his feet.

'What the hell's going on here?' he demanded before Shorty whirled and pushed him hard in the chest.

'Sit quiet you,' he commanded but the other man wasn't going to be told and again he rose. But this time a fist was driven into his solar plexus and he collapsed winded.

Shorty turned to Dooble Erchie who had been content to act as spectator only. 'Ach Erchie, if this boy's no' gaun tae behave himsel' Ah think y'd better see if big Wullie has finished his coffee.'

As the old man disappeared out of the door Alastair looked from Shorty to his wife with naked interrogation in his face. Ruth came forward to put a hand on his shoulder.

'I'm sorry love,' she said, 'even I don't know what's going to happen now.'

Before Shorty had any time to explain the door opened again and Erchie ushered in the police sergeant whom Ruth had last seen on the day of the loss of the Boy Robert. He was followed by another man who could only have been a plain clothes policeman. This man went to the window and round the opulent room then advanced to the man in the chair who was still having some trouble gathering his breath.

'Well Charlie,' he said, 'this was a bit ambitious even for you.'

He was answered with a very rude word before turning to Alastair. 'With your permission, Sir, I'd like to take this gentleman with me. The sergeant will see us to the car. I think he will then wish to come back to take a short statement from you.'

Here he looked at the sergeant who nodded before he went on. 'If you wish to press charges we will be only too happy to take them up. But please don't worry if you wish to let the matter drop. Charlie here has enough questions to answer to keep him occupied for quite some time to come.'

'Is there anything needin' done ootside?' Shorty asked as the two policemen flanked the prisoner out of the door.

Alastair laughed. 'Shorty, I don't care a damn if the place is burning down. But neither you nor Erchie get out of this room until I've heard this story. And all of it,' he added.

'We'd better maybe wait an' let Wullie huv his say first. He may be in a hurry.'

But although he was first to tell of his part in the drama haste was obviously the last thing in the mind of the big sergeant. The man who had been arrested, Charles Farquharson, was an adopted son. His parents had lived on Skye where the father had a law practice. He had launched his criminal career at the age of fifteen by stealing money from his father's office, then running away. Since then he had spent several spells in prison for theft and deception of various kinds. Several months ago he had escaped from a prison in the Midlands of England. A trail of unpaid hotel bills and bounced cheques had eventually led the police to him. He had been boasting in the bar of the hotel of how he had come to take over the estate.

Then it was Shorty's turn. He had been in the bar three evenings ago and had heard the boast. He realised that only he and Dooble Erchie had any knowledge of the background.

He had gone to seek advice from the old man. His story then bounced back over nearly half a century.

Dooble Erchie had two sisters. They had married two brothers, one of whom was Shorty's father. Just before the 14–18 war the older couple moved to Skye. The husband got a job in the mine on Raasay. A son was stillborn. The mother had been very ill after the birth and they had been told that there must be no more children.

Shorty's father had been a shepherd on the Estate but on the outbreak of war had joined the navy. Caroline Todd, who had known both men for all of her life, had gone to Glasgow to do voluntary work. She had joined a group who provided meals and rest facilities to service men in transit, from a hall close to the docks.

One day Shorty's father found his way there. His ship had been sunk off the north coast of Ireland. He was cold, hungry and filthy and had gone three days without sleep. Because of the shortage of manpower he wasn't being allowed leave but was due to join another ship at mid day on the following day. He had got married at the beginning of the war, had only had one home leave since and was desperate to get home but there was no way that this was going to be possible.

Caroline had a small flat in the Hyndland area and she had taken him there to clean up and rest. By the time he was washed and had something to eat he was dead on his feet. There was only one bed and she put him into this with the intention of sleeping, herself, in a chair. But when he was dead to the world she slipped in to the edge of the opposite side. They had both woken at the same time the following morning. Between two young people the result was inevitable and understandable.

Angus MacDonald's next home leave was seven months later. By then Caroline was home and the evidence of their indiscretion was all too obvious. Here Shorty looked towards Dooble Erchie and the older man took up the story. Whenever she was home Caroline had been in the habit of visiting Shorty's mother. At this point Shorty was around fifteen months of age. Here the uncle looked at his nephew and they both laughed. From long experience the younger man obviously knew what was coming next.

'Even noo that he's big he's still a shoart ersed wee thing. Ye can imagine whit he wis like as a stotterin' wean. My sister had kent that Caroline had met her man in Glesga an' when she saw her playin' wi' the wee fella she guessed whit had happened.'

When her husband came home she asked him outright and he immediately told her the whole story. She was an honest and practical country woman and was neither bitter nor resentful. What was really important to her was that thus far her husband had survived the war but she was concerned about the future of the child. On Caroline's next visit she offered to take the baby after it was born and bring it up as her own. The stumbling block was Caroline's father. Knowing the parentage of the baby the old laird was keen that, particularly if it was a boy, it be kept with the family and brought up as the son and heir which he would never have of his own. But then, suddenly and unexpectedly, Caroline's mother died. Into the midst of ensuing uncertainty the childless couple from Skye arrived on a visit. They pleaded to be allowed to have the baby and bring it up as their own.

'Here wis a baby that wis going tae be born oot o' wedlock. But far frae it bein' unwanted there wis a choice of three good homes.'

Caroline proved to be easier to persuade than her father. When he finally consented he wanted to settle a sum of money to help pay for the child's upbringing, but the couple didn't want this. They argued that they wanted to bring the child up as their own in an island community and extra money would maybe cause more problems than it would solve. Fortunately Shorty's father had been put on a promotion course and was still ashore. He was able to be contacted and give his approval before the baby was born. But the old laird insisted on placing a sum of money in trust to be used at the discretion of Shorty's father. 'Juist in case for some reason the coo didnae calve,' the old man ended.

Shorty again took up the narration. The baby had been born a boy. He was given his mother's surname as a middle name and when he was old enough to fully understand, this was to be explained to him. But otherwise his origins were kept as a family secret. Although many locals had been able to see that Caroline had been carrying a baby, local speculation as to its fate ranged from it having been adopted at birth to it being stillborn. The boy who came on holiday to the MacDonald's and spent time playing in the 'Big Hoose' gardens with Shorty looked so much like the MacDonald family that no one was any the wiser.

The boy had gone to Edinburgh University and had just obtained an Honours Degree when the war started and he was commissioned into the army. He had seen service in both France and the Middle East before being sent to the Far East. After the war he had gone back to Malaya but had been killed in a terrorist ambush. His adoptive parents had both died shortly afterwards.

Alastair expelled his breath when the wee man stopped speaking. 'Well,' he said, 'it's strange to think that he might have been sitting here instead of me.'

'Ah don't think he wid.' It was Dooble Erchie who spoke. 'The Laird spoke tae him at the end of the war but he wisnae interested. His plan wis tae dae a year or two mair abroad then go back tae the croft in Skye an' write books.'

'And where does Charlie Boy come in?'

It was the policeman who answered. 'He also was adopted but his adoptive parents weren't so lucky. His father had a law practice in Skye and that was where he got his information. But I'm afraid that he's nothing more than a bad lot.'

Alastair elected not to press charges but the prediction of the police sergeant proved accurate. Charlie Farquharson had escaped while he still had a year and a half of a prison sentence to serve. While on the run he had accumulated a catalogue of charges. In the end he faced a further seven years behind bars. The local police had managed to off load him without the press getting hold of the story. The Estate wasn't mentioned in court proceedings.

'Juist as well,' said Shorty. 'Ah'd have hated folk tae think that Ah had a brother lake thon.'

CHAPTER 24

When Ruth first took up her appointment she found that some patients had hived off to register with the practice in the town. This, though she regretted it, she understood. Not only was she young and black but she was also the first female doctor in the area. She had grown up in a masculine dominant society. At times this thought cracked her face in a smile since, though never aggressive, her mother could manipulate her strong father like a child moulding plasticine.

Gradually she became accepted. The fact that she enjoyed the unreserved support of her predecessor and that she continued the level of patient support which he had established meant that any detractor had difficulty in holding an audience. Strangely, the slowest converts were elderly ladies some of whom lived on their own. To them the doctor and the minister should be men. That was as it always had been and they were uncomfortable with change and the strength of opposition was directly related to the level of primness. Quite by accident, the hardest nut was cracked by a very small hammer. If Ruth was near Dooble Erchie's roadside cottage she often called in on the old man. If she was going farther up the glen she would take Heather with her, partly because she enjoyed the company but mainly because the wee dog so obviously enjoyed the car.

At the far end of the glen there was a cottage belonging to the neighbouring estate. There, lived a very serene lady. She had, in the local colloquial term, 'worked ootside', but on the death of her mother had come home to keep house for her brother who was a bachelor shepherd. On his death she had been allowed to remain in the house. Ruth had visited her several times and had always been politely received though obviously any attempt to advance the visit beyond a social occasion would have been met with rebuff.

The previous doctor hadn't recorded any problem with her. He had treated her on several occasions but never for anything serious. There was a burn about a hundred yards short of the house. Ruth left her car beside it and crossed by a wooden plank bridge. Heather splashed her way through the clear water lapping as she went. The last part of the journey to the gate in the garden wall was through a field which, in the days when a cow had been kept, had been a hay meadow.

The sopranino calls of circling lapwings told Ruth that there were chicks hidden in the long grass and she ordered Heather to stay close to her but as they neared the garden wall the dog became increasingly agitated and tried to run ahead. Then Ruth became aware of another cry which was penetrating even the high pitched noise of the birds. She stopped to listen and in that bowl surrounded by dark hills she felt the flesh crawl on the back of her neck. From beyond the stone wall there was emanating a howl of excruciating agony. She ran towards the noise. Miss MacBeth was just inside the gate half sitting, half lying with her back against the wall. The front of her cream blouse was covered in drying grainy blood like black sawdust, which she had recently vomited.

When she saw the tall black doctor the howl stopped. She tried to speak, retched and a foam of red spittle appeared at her lips. Because of her reception on previous visits Ruth had left her bag in the car but in this case it would have done little good. She knelt to take a pulse and with her other hand smoothed back mousy grey hair from the hot sticky brow. Heather moved round to sit on the other side of the patient. The pulse was slow and slightly irregular.

'Miss MacBeth, can you hear me?'

There was a nod of a head in which the teeth were clenched.

'I'm going to get you to hospital. But first I'll run to the car to get you an injection which will dull your pain before I move you.'

When she returned she found that Heather had moved close and long slim fingers were gently moving over the wiry hair of the terrier. More surprisingly this prim lady had pulled up her skirt on one side and eased down her pants far enough to allow access to an injection site on her hip.

'We'll give that a minute or two to get to work,' said Ruth when she pressed home the plunger. 'Now can you tell me where to find a toilet bag and nightie?'

'Waste of time,' the first words from the patient were clipped by pain. 'I'll never reach Glasgow.'

'But you're not going to Glasgow. We have a surgeon in Campbeltown now. He was a student with me. He's good. His name is George MacKenzie.'

The strained features relaxed a little.

'Bathroom and chest of drawers in my bedroom. Dressing gown on the bed. Small case under the bed. Don't lock the door. No need.'

As she ran the short distance to the house Ruth realised that Miss MacBeth hadn't asked the usual question as to what was wrong with her.

The two bedrooms were at the top of a steep wooden stair and had wood-lined, sloping ceilings,. The first door that Ruth opened was tidy but austere, a man's room cared for by a woman. There was the slight musty odour of disuse which no amount of airing can totally dispel.

Behind the other door there was the boudoir of a fastidious lady. The floor space wasn't large and the slope of the ceiling allowed just enough height for the head of the bed to be tucked to the wall. Despite the need for haste Ruth paused for a minute. The decoration was in pastel shades and carefully chosen to blend yet brighten like primroses on the bank of a burn. Between the bed and the chest of drawers which backed to the gable wall a kidney shaped dressing table with a swing mirror was angled so that someone sitting on the stool could catch the light from the deep-silled dormer window.

The top of the dressing table was bare except for a framed photograph of a young man in the uniform of an RAF officer.

The photograph stood slightly in shade but had been taken in a good light. The aquiline features carried a strength unusual in one so young and despite being out of the strongest light the photograph dominated the room to the extent that as Ruth gathered things to put in the case she felt that the eyes were following her.

Not daring to disturb the pristine condition of the bed Ruth snatched two pillows from the other room before hurrying back to the garden. Miss MacBeth had shed some of the disjointed rag doll look. Heather was sitting close and she was speaking to the dog as she stroked her.

'I'll just leave these things in the car. Be back in a tick,' Ruth told her.

After reclining the passenger seat and arranging the pillows she got back to find that her patient had struggled to her feet and was using both hands to gain support from the wall.

'Can you walk?'

'Yes,' but the voice was strained and hesitant.

Slowly, with Ruth's arm around her waist they passed through the gap in the wall, But as Ruth reached to latch the gate she relaxed her arm and Miss MacBeth crumpled to the ground.

Ruth crouched, pulled the left arm round her own neck, passed her right arm round the shoulders, her left arm under the knees and taking all the weight on her legs, lifted her patient. It was done so swiftly and with such fluidity of movement that there was no time for protest. When protest did find a voice it was struggling against pain.

'You can't carry me like this. I'm too heavy.'

The imp in Ruth couldn't resist it. 'Would you like me to take you on my head?' she said smiling into the white face.

Miss MacBeth blushed. 'I'm sorry. I was wrong. Forgive me.'

Ruth tightened her arms in the nearest to a hug which the circumstances allowed.

'I'll stop at Marie Sinclair's to leave Heather and phone the hospital,' said Ruth as they neared the bottom of the glen.

Miss MacBeth had been sick as she was arranged in the car but had travelled fairly well as Ruth struggled to balance the need for haste with the comfort of her patient. Marie was working in her garden and came forward smiling.

But the smile vanished when she saw the stretched out figure in the car. Hastily Ruth explained but as she turned to go to the phone she heard a voice behind her. 'My blood group is A Negative.'

As Ruth hurried round the corner she realised that she hadn't yet told the patient what was wrong with her. And the patient still hadn't asked. By the time she got back to the car Miss MacBeth had her eyes closed. Marie's interrogative look was answered with a shake of the head.

'I don't know,' said Ruth. 'I just don't know.'

Two miles on in the speeding car she glanced over her shoulder to realise that Heather was still in the car. She lay close to her new found friend and gently licked her hand. At each stroke of her tongue the fingers of the hand flexed. But by the time they reached the hospital Miss MacBeth was unconscious. George MacKenzie met Ruth in the foyer of the hospital as two porters wheeled in a trolley. He took a quick glance at the pallid face then said 'Theatre – right away' before turning to her doctor.

'Perforated duodenum, I think,' she quickly answered his question before he had time to ask it.

'How recent?'

'Under two hours. But only just.'

'We should still have a chance,' and he hurried after the trolley.

As Ruth drove home through the busy harvest fields her mind dwelt with the patient she had left and she wondered about the story behind this prim middle aged lady. Normally, Heather travelled on the back seat and at times on the rear parcel tray. But as Ruth had brought up the reclined front passenger seat the dog jumped over to establish herself in the seat-well in the front of the car. When they were out on the quiet, flat road Ruth snapped her fingers and patted the seat beside her. Heather jumped up to lie on the seat with her chin resting on her front paws. Ruth, driving with one hand, placed the splayed fingers of the other hand on the dog's head and fondled her ears. Ruth felt that without the little dog her job would have been much more difficult. Somehow the presence of Heather had given the impression that she wasn't alone and had given confidence.

Miss MacBeth was very ill indeed and her survival depended partly on the skill of George MacKenzie and partly on her own will to live but there was hope in the fact that she had volunteered her blood group.

Who was the young man whose photograph dominated the bedroom to the extent that you felt that he was present? Were there relatives who should be notified? Miss MacBeth was the one patient on whom Dr Marshall had left the most cursory of notes.

Obviously she had been more antagonistic towards Ruth than Ruth herself had realised. Was this because she was black or just the fairly common antipathy towards 'lassie doctors' which thankfully was disappearing? Or was her attitude simply a defence of her privacy? The family didn't belong to the area so there was no local knowledge.

Part of Ruth's own early acceptance was due to her friendship with the Sinclairs. Then her early successes coupled with the enthusiastic endorsement of her predecessor gained her favours as a doctor. Then she had married the laird whose family had been good landlords and considerate employers. Miss MacBeth had enjoyed none of these advantages.

Alastair and Ruth had just finished their evening meal when George MacKenzie phoned.

'The operation went well but it's early days as yet,' he told Ruth. 'But she's very agitated. She wants to see you. Could you possibly come in? I doubt if we can get her to settle until she has spoken to you.'

'I'll drive you,' said Alastair when she told him where she was going.

Miss MacBeth was restless and obviously in pain. Ruth

drew in the visitor's chair, sat and took her hand. 'Am I going to die?' The voice was surprisingly strong.

Ruth hesitated just for a moment. 'I've spoken to Mr MacKenzie. He thinks that your chances are good.'

The eyes swung away for a moment then came back. 'I think my son should know. If I give you a number would you telephone him?'

Ruth struggled to keep the surprise from her voice. 'Of course. I'll phone from here.'

A deep, calm voice answered her call. She explained who she was and why she was phoning. There was silence for a second or two then 'Would you advise that I drive up tonight? I could be there in about five hours.'

Ruth paused in turn. 'How long is it since you slept?'

There came a short, rather rueful chuckle. 'I rose at five this morning.'

'Then my advice is to get a night's sleep. You will not help your mother by risking a long night drive when you are tired. And be assured, everything that can be done for your mother is being done.'

'Thank you Doctor. Tell my mother that I love her. I'll see her tomorrow.'

Having finished morning surgery Ruth was clearing her desk when a shadow darkened the door.

'Dr MacIntyre?'

'Yes.'

'I'm Bruce MacBeth and this is my wife, Deborah.'

Deborah MacBeth was tall, blond and beautiful. Her husband was also tall with thick black hair. His surprise on seeing Ruth was only matched by her surprise at sight of him. Bruce MacBeth's strong, handsome features were of a rich golden brown colour which owed nothing to any recent effect of the sun.

CHAPTER 25

The couple stayed for just under a week and by that time Miss MacBeth was well on the road to recovery. She was obviously very proud of her son and the prompt visit of he and his wife had helped her immensely. It wasn't until she was settled at home that Ruth heard the story. Deborah had told her that she and Bruce were both research scientists who had met while at university. They had been married for just over a year.

On a dour autumn afternoon Ruth left her car to walk across the bridge and up through the meadow. The lowered arc of the sun had prevented it from touching here and the grass was still covered in white frost from the morning. The sky was clouding over from the west and Ruth shivered as she reached the door but inside she found a room brightened by a cheerful fire. Miss MacBeth had seen the car come up the other side of the glen and a tea tray sat on a small table. On the arm of the chair where she had been sitting an open Angus MacVicar novel lay face down and on the sideboard the flickering flames of the fire darted off the strong features of the photograph which Ruth had last seen in the upstairs bedroom.

Miss MacBeth was obviously well. She had taken time with her hair and her makeup was done with that clever subtlety which made it difficult to decide if she was wearing any. Despite herself, Ruth found her glance being drawn to the face in the photograph.

Their cups were topped up, the teapot placed in the hearth close to the fire. The hostess sat back comfortably in her chair and smiled.

'Do you like my choice in young men?'

'I do indeed.' Ruth was slightly embarrassed.

'That was my fiancé. He was a Battle of Britain pilot. A bullet severed an hydraulic pipe during a dogfight and the undercarriage of his plane wouldn't come down. When he tried to land it burst into flames.'

There was a silence broken only by the guttering of the fire in the grate before she went on.

'I was staff nurse in a hospital in Chelmsford and was on duty when they brought him in there.' Another pause then 'I didn't recognise him. The strap of his helmet had broken in the crash. His face was just a charred mass and his hair had burnt off. He lived for almost three hours. Just before he died the Padre from his unit came to the hospital. It was only then that we found out who he was. I tried to speak to him but couldn't tell if he could hear me. I couldn't even hold his hand because of the burns.'

Quietly she lifted her cup, took a sip of tea and replaced the cup in her saucer.

'When John died I just felt empty. I wasn't alone. Many of the girls that I worked with had lost their men. There just wasn't time for grief so I joined the Queen Alexandra Nursing Corps and went to do field hospital work in North Africa.'

'Then we were sent back to Weymouth to prepare for the D-day landings. One of the team was a black surgeon who had been born in Liverpool. We became friendly. I suppose he was in love with me but if I loved him it wasn't the same as it had been with John. He was a kind, gentle man and a brilliant surgeon.'

'He was to go over with the first wave of troops and the rest of the unit was to follow. We didn't know the exact date but realised that it had to be very soon. One night we went for a walk on the beach. It was a beautiful early June night and we lay among the dunes. David sailed two nights later.'

'When they were running up the beach he went to help a soldier who had been shot. The man had been about to throw a hand grenade when he had fallen. When David turned him over it exploded. Two months later, in northern France, I realised that I was pregnant.'

She bent to lift a poker to push in a piece of coal that was threatening to fall on the hearth.

'To this day I don't know whether or not I did it deliberately. After John died I wished that I had his baby as a part of him to keep. Maybe I thought that I wasn't going to see David again. Or it may be, Doctor, that I was just a common slut.'

'Miss MacBeth, I have been a woman for longer than I have been a doctor. And if you were a common slut I would have been the same in similar circumstances. And you have every reason to be proud of your son.'

Before Alastair and Ruth got married they had decided to wait a while before starting a family. Mainly it was Alastair's idea.

'You'll have plenty to cope with without a baby as well,' he told Ruth.

But as, warmly cocooned in her car, she slowly made her way down the chatter mark surface of the glen road Ruth decided that it was now time for things to change. She smiled to herself as she remembered something her mother had told her on the day when she had become a wife.

'At times it is best not to tell men too much. Their heads are filled with so many important things that something really important can get lost in the jumble. If you can do something on your own, just get on with it. If your man needs to know he'll find out soon enough. But always make sure that whatever you do is to his benefit.'

This she couldn't do on her own. But it certainly would be to Alastair's benefit. She would like to have a gentleman's family. A son like Bruce MacBeth. A daughter like Sarah. Both were children of mixed race and both were extraordinarily handsome and attractive.

Months succeeded other winter months and found their way into a cold late spring. Alastair and his men struggled through a difficult lambing time of ewes in poor condition. This not only meant that mothers had little milk for newborn lambs but had a follow on effect on natural mothering instinct particularly in the younger ewes.

Alastair was permanently tired and, unusually for him, became irritable and snappy. Shorty, despite being much older, seemed indestructible. Fostering each day's crop of orphaned lambs on unwilling mothers meant that invariably the shadows were lengthening before he climbed into the Land Rover to head for home. Yet, daylight was barely a promise in the eastern sky when his cheerful whistle could again be heard.

The sunless, cheerless weather also brought an increase in work and frustration for Ruth. Both the very young and the very old were being brought low by relatively simply malaise that normally they would have shrugged off. Even the indefectible Mrs MacGregor was forced to bed for a few days with a flu like illness.

Then suddenly the skies cleared, the sun shone and the swallows returned to the eaves. Full bellied lambs played their own version of King of the Castle along turf dykes. On a bright Saturday morning in early June Ruth packed a picnic haversack and she and Alastair climbed the hill to walk the ridges towards the Eagles Rock.

At first it was uncomfortably hot but as they gained height they picked up sufficient breeze to make conditions very pleasant. At the top they paused to catch their breath and admire the view. Geographically, they stood almost in the centre of the part of the estate which Alastair farmed himself. In the middle distance to the east could be seen the steadings of three farms that were tenanted.

Ruth moved close to Alastair and took his hand. He released her grip and put his arm around her shoulders. They were draped in the sounds of early summer. An inquisitive lamb sniffed at a clump of blue gentian. Its mother grazed busily a few yards away. A bee, which had been carrying out its own investigation of the flowers flew out startling the lamb. Its sudden backward movement transmitted itself to the ewe and she gave a short, gurgling bleat. The lamb ran and dived beneath her to suckle. As it butted her vessel to stimulate the let down of milk the hind leg of the ewe was lifted off the ground. The mother sniffed the lamb to reassure herself then started to chew her cud.

'Do you recognise her?' Alastair asked, nodding towards the ewe.

'No. Should I?'

'Well, you cursed her for eating the crocuses. Shorty had her tethered on the lawn for nearly a week before he persuaded her to mother that lamb.'

On the rounded crown of the hill the going was easier and they joined hands for a time as they continued westwards. Ahead, the sun lanced off the blue waves of the Atlantic. To their right, Islay lay cleanly in the water but a wispy cap of mist crowned the Paps of Jura.

As they breasted the hill at the Eagles Rock the pristine white of the Mull of Kintyre lighthouse shone almost a thousand feet below them. But even on that calm day the meeting of the tides produced a turbulence which caused a puffer to plunge like an unbroken horse on its first taste of a restraining halter.

Ruth felt Alastair's hand on her arm and he pointed ahead and slightly to their right. At first she couldn't see what he was indicating Then the sun glinted on the eye of a grouse. After a moment or two more she could pick out five chicks frozen in the short heather where they had been busily feeding before the frightening intrusion of the man and woman.

Silently they moved off to the left. They had gone a bare fifty yards when there was a sudden sharp noise behind them. They turned, horrified, to see a golden eagle rising with the adult grouse clutched, dead, in its talons.

'Oh, Alastair. The chicks. We must do something.'

'There's nothing we can do except hope that they are old enough to survive on their own. Pheasant chicks can be reared like domestic chickens. But nobody has ever found a way to do that with grouse.'

By the time they entered the small hollow where they had picnicked on the day when they became engaged, Ruth had tears running openly down her cheeks. Alastair shrugged off the haversack and took her in his arms.

She dropped her head to his chest and sobbed. After a time she lifted a tear stained face to look into the level eyes of this strong, honest, big man with whom she was sharing her life.

They kissed deeply, then sank to the warm, green, inviting grass.

Samuel Alastair MacIntyre was born early on a bright March morning. Dr Marshall and Margaret Thompson, who was now Margaret MacKay and expecting a baby of her own, attended. The old man was particularly pleased.

'I've delivered babies in every house in the district and also in a fair number of tinkers' tents but this is the first in the Big Hoose,' he said.

'We'll call him Sam,' said Ruth when she looked at the round, golden features of her son.